"When are you going to grow up, Margot?"

Adam was facing her aggressively, long legs spread, hands thrust into the pockets of his sheepskin jacket. "You'll be twenty in a few months."

"Who says I'll ever reach twenty?" Margot responded with a sneer, more for effect than anything else.

Her words made his handsome face tighten with real anger. Strong fingers grasped her sweater, jerking her forward in a teeth-jarring motion. His intensity was frightening, and her face whitened as he glared fiercely into her eyes that were only inches away. "Don't *ever* let me hear you speak like that again," he said savagely. "You're *not* worthless! You're precious, can't you understand that?"

"You're hurting me," she whispered. "And just who am I precious to?"

She saw his eyes glitter just before he pulled her close, claiming her for his own....

MADELEINE KER is a self-described "compulsive writer." In fact, Madeleine has been known to deliver six romances in less than a year. The author is married, and in addition to a writing career, she is a graduate student at Durham University.

Books by Madeleine Ker

HARLEQUIN PRESENTS

HARLEQUIN ROMANCE

Don't miss any of our special offers. Write to us at the following address for information on our newest releases.

Harlequin Reader Service
901 Fuhrmann Blvd., P.O. Box 1397, Buffalo, NY 14240
Canadian address: P.O. Box 603,
Fort Erie, Ont. L2A 5X3

MADELEINE KER

the wilder shores of love

Harlequin Books

TORONTO • NEW YORK • LONDON
AMSTERDAM • PARIS • SYDNEY • HAMBURG
STOCKHOLM • ATHENS • TOKYO • MILAN

Harlequin Presents first edition October 1988
ISBN 0-373-11114-2

Original hardcover edition published in 1987
by Mills & Boon Limited

CHAPTER ONE

HE MUST have been standing in the street all the time she was in the dealer's house, though she hadn't noticed him.

She'd been feeling ill, of course. Every day it seemed to come on sooner, more urgently, a build-up of fear and hunger that she couldn't fight.

That was partly why she'd been careless.

Not that it really mattered, for even if she had noticed him that afternoon, and had managed to take evasive action of some kind, he would simply have waited for another time and another place.

As it was, she was only half aware of the man who was standing by the glossy black railings as she walked down the stairs from the smartly modernised Victorian house, the little white packet safely hidden in her bag.

The chill autumn wind swept her dark hair momentarily across her face, a sweetly oval, nineteen-year-old face that sometimes held the mysterious calm of a madonna's, but which was now pale and troubled.

In the severe black coat, Margot Prescott seemed almost frail. The beautiful lines of her temples, cheekbones and throat were emphasised as much by her pallor as by the weight she'd lost recently. Had she worn make-up to accentuate a full mouth and sloe-black eyes, she might have been strikingly beautiful, even dramatically so. A little make-up would also have made it even harder to tell that the frail quality was real, not assumed.

She stepped past the railings on long, elegant legs. Her

mind was already concentrating itself on where she could safely take the first quarter. She needed it badly. She'd left it far too long, out of some stupid bravado. Kidding herself she didn't have to rush. She was starting to feel terrible.

When the tall man took her arm firmly, she felt shock squeeze her heart.

'One moment.'

She gave a little gasp. 'Yes?'

He was tall, in a beautiful fawn Burberry. She didn't recognise him at all; it was a sophisticated, intensely masculine face, but also a dangerous face. The grey eyes were most dangerous of all. Against the burned-honey tan of his skin, they were as clear and deep as Alpine lake water. You could sink into them, lose yourself in their depths.

'Give it to me, please.'

'Give you wh-what?'

He smiled, but it didn't touch his eyes. 'October weather isn't good enough to waste time in, Margot. The heroin. Give it to me, please.'

He knew her name. A professional, then. Narcotics Squad. Oh *hell*.

Margot had no strength to argue. Feeling despair wash over her, she fumbled in her bag and passed him the package.

He weighed it briefly in his palm, the icy eyes holding hers so compellingly that she couldn't look away. 'A gram?' he asked. Margot nodded, feeling sick to her heart.

He didn't glance at the package, just twisted it open between finger and thumb, and scattered the white powder on to the grass underfoot.

She whimpered at the waste, feeling the need clawing viciously at her nerves. Then, as realisation dawned, she turned to him with a twisted smile.

'There's your evidence gone, at any rate.' Margot drew a shaky breath, meeting the assessing eyes. 'You've got nothing on me now, have you?' She'd really thought she was going to be arrested, and her legs were wobbly with delayed shock. She tried to pull her arm free. But either he was numbingly strong, or there was no resistance left in her muscles.

'Let me go!'

'Not just yet.'

The smoky-smooth voice had a husky undercurrent. She wasn't so sure about him, now. He didn't have a policeman's style, and a policeman's salary didn't extend to the kind of clothes he was wearing.

'Who are you?' she asked tightly.

'We need to talk,' he said easily. 'My car's just around the block.' The thick black hair had been cut in Curzon Street, with no attempt to minimise the distinguished silver streaks that put his age at somewhere in his early thirties. It was the unmistakable authority in his face, though, that marked him as infinitely older, more powerful than she.

'I—I have an appointment.'

'No, you haven't,' he contradicted, as though the idea amused him.

'Let me go,' she challenged unsteadily, 'or I'll scream——'

'Now, now.' He turned her around to face down the street. There was a police car parked a few hundred yards away. 'There are two efficient young bobbies in that car, praying for something exciting to happen,' he said gently. 'I'm sure they'd be very interested in you—not to mention your pharmaceutical friend in the upstairs flat.'

Numbly, she let him walk her to the intersection. 'Are you—are you a dealer?' she asked.

'Come on.' His eyes glittered. 'Do I look like that kind of filth? Just keep walking, Margot.'

'H-how do you know my name?'

'It means "pearl".' He was still smiling, escorting her along with the easy grace of a lover, nothing to indicate that there was any compulsion involved. 'I've always loved the name. A pearl from the wilder shores of love.' He confused her. The bring-down of seeing the heroin scattered had brought her need leaping up into her throat, like a raging thirst. The pain was starting again, sharper along the branches of her nerves. She wanted a fix. Now.

'Who the hell are you?'

'Don't waste your time struggling.' She was still feebly trying to wrest her arm loose from his grasp. 'I don't intend you any harm.' But there was an assured power about every move he made which told her he was going to have his way with her, no matter what his intentions were.

Four o'clock on a Friday afternoon in late autumn, the sun setting through the trees in the park, an orange streak dying in the promise of a wet weekend. A light spattering of rain drifted into her face. It was all becoming dreamlike, everything except the relentless build-up of need in her.

They crossed, still arm-in-arm towards the car park.

'Get in the car, please.'

It was an anthracite-grey Mercedes coupé with tinted glass and a private registration-plate. Anonymous and fast. Margot stopped in her tracks, resisting the smooth power of his arm with real alarm. 'Where exactly are you taking me? You haven't shown me any kind of identification!'

The smile he gave her was mocking. 'Be fair. Have I asked *you* for identification?' He was between her and the opened door of the Mercedes now, blocking her escape. The man moved with the economical precision of an expert doing something very familiar. There was unmistakable menace in the pantherine smoothness of his movements. 'Get in.' The car park was almost empty but for whirling leaves. She had no choice but to obey.

Unashamedly, he studied her legs as she swung them over the sill. 'You should have been a dancer, pearl.'

He slammed the door shut on her, imprisoning her in the luxuriously scented interior. Numbly, she saw that there was no opening button on her door. Panic flooded her, tightening her lungs in an iron grip, but it took him only seconds to stride round the car and slide into the driver's seat beside her. 'Please tell me who you are,' she said, her voice uneven.

'I'm a friend.'

She searched his face again for some glimmer of familiarity, but there was none. It was completely strange to her; alien, male and harsh.

Margot tried to keep her voice level, her tone reasonable. She needed to stay calm. 'My friends don't treat me like this.' She should have called his bluff about the police. People who used heroin were frighteningly vulnerable. But she'd been too disorientated to really understand what was happening to her. 'I can't remember ever having met you in my life!'

'That isn't important right now.' He started the car, and drove out of the deserted car park.

At the end of Ovenstone Terrace he turned into the arterial route through North London. At four o'clock on this Friday evening, the traffic was building up steadily.

'How are you feeling?' he asked, scattering too-slow pedestrians with ruthless skill.

Margot's throat was dry enough to make swallowing painful. 'I want to be out of here,' she said huskily. Her fingers clenched round the door handle in a spasm of claustrophobia. 'I don't feel well.'

'You're going to feel worse,' he informed her calmly. 'You might as well start getting used to it.'

Get lost, she thought savagely, but kept the words to herself. 'Where exactly are you taking me?' she demanded, aloud.

'You've won a free holiday for one in the heart of the country.' He didn't even look at her as he accelerated smoothly through a gap in the traffic. 'You're going to love it. Try and relax. Recite a mantra.'

'Don't treat me like a child!' she snapped with a flash of anger. She abandoned her futile effort to open the door, and huddled into her wool coat. She could scarcely believe what had happened in the past few minutes; she'd been picked up and blown along like a leaf in a gale. 'Why are you interfering in my life?'

'Your life,' he repeated with irony smooth as a razor's edge. 'Well, it's been such a dazzling success so far that I thought I'd stop you and find out your secret.'

She turned to him, passion flaring smokily in her dark eyes. 'How *dare* you talk to me like that?'

'Ah.' He spared her a coolly mocking glance. 'So there is life after heroin addiction.'

'I'm not an addict!'

But Margot's moment of courage was already draining away as the anxiety rose. Every nerve was beginning to tighten like the strings of a tormented violin. It would take a few more hours for the misery to really take hold. She knew, from the times she'd tried to give heroin up. Unsuccessfully.

She stared out of the window at the rainy autumn streets. The shiny pavements and bright shops were still crowded with last-minute shoppers. This was like a dream. Like being in a film. Watching some plot unfold around yourself, and not knowing where on earth it would all lead.

What did you do in a situation like this? Scream and kick, and try to make him crash the car? She wasn't frantic enough for that. It wasn't just that her emotions were flat and colourless these days, the drug preventing her from feeling anything properly; the man beside her had handled her with the ease of a master horseman—no fuss, no bother. And no possibility of resistance.

The faces in the cars around them were incurious, intent on getting home to hot dinners in the suburbs. It occurred to her vaguely that she could bang on the glass, wave frantically for help, but somehow she knew she would only look absurd—even if anyone were to notice her through the tinted glass of the Mercedes.

So she sat in silence, with nothing to say, and kept staring out of the window. Within ten minutes, she had started to shiver, despite the warmth of the car. An icy cold was starting to take her in a vice-like grip.

'Here.' Without taking his eyes off the road, he passed her a small tortoiseshell box. Inside were two innocent-looking white tablets, like aspirins.

'Wha——' She swallowed painfully. 'What are they?'

'Peppermints. Arsenic. Does it matter?'

'Of *course* it matters!'

'It's physeptone. Take it.'

'What's physeptone?'

'You'd probably know it as Methadone.'

Her fingers were shaking as she picked the pills up. She knew that they would bring relief. It was used to help addicts come off hard drugs. Margot felt the nausea rising inside. She wanted to fling the tablets away, curse him. Tell him she didn't need the damned stuff. But there was no way she could refuse them.

She took the pills, her throat dry, and lay back, closing her eyes in exhaustion. The Methadone helped to place him, at any rate. It was a drug associated with hospitals, therapeutic communities, that kind of thing. Do-gooders.

'You've lost weight,' he commented in that smooth, matter-of-fact way he had.

'How do you know?' she enquired.

'Your father showed me pictures of you.'

'Oh . . .' Surprise flickered in her. 'Did you know him?'

'I was a friend.'

'Were you?' She rubbed her aching temples with her fingertips, her mind struggling with this new line of thought. 'What's your name?'

'Adam Korda.'

'Adam Korda . . .' There had been so many people who'd had contacts with her father. She couldn't pick this man's face or name out of the fresh pain of her memory. Maybe, at least, he wasn't a psychopath or a rapist. But who the hell was he, then? 'What does all this have to do with my father?' Margot demanded, pulling her coat close around her shivering body.

He smiled slightly. 'Let's say I'm doing something on his behalf. Something I think he would have done himself if he hadn't died.' The muscles of his thigh pulsed as he had to brake hard. 'Women drivers,' he muttered, and swung the wheel to overtake an erring Fiat.

'Something he would have done . . . An attempt to wean me away from my wicked ways?' she asked drily, studying his tanned profile.

'That's not a bad assessment.'

'Ah . . .' Understanding started to dawn out of the darkness. Was *that* what this extraordinary charade was leading to? 'I begin to see. And where exactly are you taking me? Some kind of drug rehabilitation centre, I presume.'

'Something like that,' he agreed.

Thank God.

For the first time since she'd got into the car, Margot unclenched her fists. Her hands were clammy, little half-moons cut into the palms by frightened fingernails. Pent-up fear started to ebb away now, and she slumped back. 'You scared me half to death, Mr Adam Korda,' she said with a little gasp of laughter. 'I thought I was being dragged off to some horrible fate. Is this the way you always do business?'

'When the occasion calls for it,' he said calmly. 'Drowning people sometimes put up quite a struggle.'

'Oh, how bloody ridiculous,' she said tiredly. 'Just because someone has a couple of drinks, you don't call Alcoholics Anonymous!'

'There's a certain qualitative difference between a couple of drinks and a budding heroin habit,' he said mildly, pushing a tape into the radio-cassette-player.

'I've told you, I'm not an addict!'

'Find a euphemism, then,' he said with a hint of mature amusement she didn't like. 'User? Dependent?'

'What I do with my life is my own business,' she said sullenly. She studied the animal quality that lurked in the corners of his eyes, his nostrils, the slant of his mouth. He was used to commanding other men, that was evident in every line. 'Just who do you imagine you are?' she sneered. 'The white knight rescuing the damsel from the dragon?'

'In this case, the dragon is white,' he said calmly. 'And the damsel appears to be too stupid to know she's in distress.'

Another angry retort had risen to her lips, but a languorous calm was stealing through her veins now. The Methadone was making her float, leaving everything behind her. She sighed, tense shoulders relaxing as the pain of heroin withdrawal eased away.

He glanced at her quickly. 'Feeling better?'

Margot nodded, her hostility almost gone now. 'Very tired.'

'Then sleep. My driving terrifies most people anyway, and it's a long journey. There's a rug on the back seat.'

She fumbled for the warm woollen travelling rug, and huddled into its comfort. The floating sensation was gathering force, making everything else seem unimportant. Margot rolled her head back against the seat with another sigh. The drug was strong. 'Are they expecting me at this ... nursing home?'

'Yes.'

'I don't *want* to go!' The Methadone had softened her diction, slurred it, and it was hard to inject any real anger into her voice. 'I've got a choice, you know. This isn't Nazi Germany. And I don't want to go to this place!'

'You haven't seen it yet,' he pointed out.

'It's completely mad,' she groaned. 'What have you told them ... about me?'

'That you need help.'

She snorted. 'And you expect me to drop everything and go on some kind of rest-cure? Just how long are you expecting me to stay?'

'There's no hurry,' he said gently, glancing out of the window at the golden glimmering of the sunset. 'You don't have any pressing engagements, do you?'

Margot felt disquiet rise inside her, despite the Methadone, like a fish rising to the surface of a dark pool. Damn him, she thought numbly. He knew more about her than she liked. He was taking her to some unknown place, to be treated by unknown people. If only she could clear her mind. But the Methadone was making her float away from it all, loosening the sinews of her mind. She couldn't keep her eyes open.

'Mr Korda——'

'Adam.'

'Adam, then. I suppose you think you're doing something very ... noble and worthwhile. You're only wasting your time ... and mine. I don't need anyone's help.'

'No?'

'No,' she echoed, hearing the irony in his tone. 'As soon as you drop me off there,' she told him sleepily, 'I'm going to walk straight out ... and get the first train or bus back home.'

'I don't think so.'

Something in the quiet way he said it made her open her eyes momentarily. 'You know,' she complained, with a last flash of sharpness, 'I don't think I've ever met anyone so damned sure of himself in my life.'

'No,' he said calmly, 'I don't suppose you have.'

She couldn't fight the Methadone any longer, it was far too strong. She felt the welcoming wings of sleep folding around her, and drifted into the darkness.

* * *

'God, it's cold.'

The words were just a whimper. She'd been curled up on the seat with her legs drawn up, and it was only when she was fully awake that she realised that the tall man and the grey car hadn't been a dream.

It was dark, the Mercedes' brilliant headlamps stabbing along a hedgerow-lined country road. The rim of the moon glittered silver high above the trees.

She could still feel the Methadone in her system, and she sat up stiffly. Adam's face was dimly lit by the glow from the dashboard instruments, and she caught the glint of his eyes as he glanced her way.

'I thought I heard you stir. How are you feeling?'

'Not very good,' Margot said huskily. 'How long have I been asleep?'

'Three or four hours.' A strong hand reached for her wrist, fingers seeking the warm pulse of life there. She let him measure it in silence. She should have stayed awake. She was in the hands of a man who might well be crazy, despite his claims, or dangerous, or both.

He touched her forehead. 'You're getting a temperature.'

Margot rubbed her icy arms, huddling into the rug. 'I'm so cold. Can't you turn up the heating?'

'It's hot enough in here,' he contradicted. 'Any hotter and you're going to start melting. The cold is inside you.'

Considering the power of the Mercedes, they could be almost anywhere in England by now. 'Where are we?' she asked. 'Is there much further to go?'

'Only a few more miles.'

Good, she thought grimly. As soon as she could see a doctor, someone in authority, she'd tell them she was there under compulsion. She'd insist she be taken back to

London immediately. There would be hell to pay when she informed them how she'd been virtually kidnapped there. Restlessly, she demanded, 'Who's in charge of this—this place?'

'Time enough to sort that out when we arrive,' he replied. His profile was dark, but she remembered Adam Korda's brilliant grey eyes and commanding mouth all too well.

She shook her head, suddenly aware that she was crumpled and cramped after the hours in the car. She was going to be meeting people, soon. She mustn't give the impression of being a squalid junkie.

She found her brush in her bag, and tried to comb her hair into a semblance of order. He'd probably told them to expect a hopeless addict, and she'd enjoy making Mr Korda look a fool. She also found her perfume, and sprayed icy clouds on to her throat and wrists. The car filled with the flowery smell of *Diorissima*.

She sensed, rather than heard, his chuckle.

'What's so funny?' she demanded irritably.

'You're all woman,' he said, still smiling. 'I like that fragrance. What is it?'

'You know everything else about me,' she commented acidly, 'I'm surprised you don't know that.'

The headlights lit up a crossroads. She was too late to catch the names on the signposts, except one: Harcourt. She'd never heard of it. A tiny village, probably.

The thought suddenly struck her that the Methadone would eventually wear off, and that she'd been a long time without heroin. If she didn't get a fix, a proper fix, she'd soon be in bad trouble.

Would they give her something at the place? Damn! Her insistence that she wasn't an addict would be rather tarnished by a request for drugs. Besides, medical people were reluctant to give heroin out to addicts, she knew that from her research into the drugs scene.

But they'd have to give her something. Wouldn't they? She put the perfume back into her bag. Too bad about that good impression. She didn't have any choice; she'd *have* to ask them to give her something …

About half a mile onwards, they reached a broad pair of wrought-iron gates. With electronic obedience, they swung apart to let the Mercedes purr through into the estate beyond.

Margot sat in silence, straining her eyes to catch glimpses of the parkland they were driving through. The towering shapes of great trees loomed in the headlights, beyond the tangled walls of rhododendrons that lined the drive. An owl swooped silently across their path, and was gone in the inky blackness.

This was a very exclusive institution, judging by the grounds alone. But there were no signs of human life at all, no lights, no cars or buildings. Only a large sign every few hundred yards, warning; 'Please Drive Slowly—Horses'.

Suddenly she gasped, her eyes widening to take in the ghostly shapes of a dozen deer crossing the road ahead of them. Adam stopped the car, and Margot watched in silent awe as the beautiful russet creatures passed through the light of the headlamps.

The stag, a magnificent animal with antlers like many-branched candelabra, followed in the rear. He paused for a moment, majestic in the light, his eyes shining silver as he stared at the car. In the magic of the moment, she even forgot the gnawing pain that was building up inside.

Then, breathtakingly graceful, he sprang into the dark, and was gone.

'What is this place?' Margot asked in a whisper as the car started forward again. 'Is it really a drug rehabilitation centre?'

'Indeed. We're nearly at the lodge.'

The headlights swept along the façade of a stone-built cottage set among venerable beeches. There were no lights showing. Adam stopped, and reversed towards the cottage.

'Is *this* it?' Margot asked, craning her neck to see through the darkness.

'We're home,' he agreed easily. He pulled up on the gravel, switched off the engine, and while she stared at him speechlessly, he stretched his powerful shoulders with a deep, quiet sigh. 'Home, sweet home.'

'But—but there's no one here!'

'There is now.' He unlocked her door, but Margot was in no hurry to move. Shock was still spreading through her.

'There *is* a hospital somewhere, isn't there?' she said, almost pleadingly.

'Come on.' He opened the door and swung his tall frame out.

Feeling stiff and horribly weak, she let herself out. The evening air was cool, making her shiver. Adam was taking two large pigskin suitcases from the boot. He slammed the lid down, and led her towards the ivy-fringed front door.

'This is a bad dream,' she whispered, looking at the deserted cottage. Her notions of impressing an awaiting staff were fading rapidly. 'It must be. What in God's name are we going to do here?'

'See a lot of each other, for one thing.' Bright lights flicked on, illuminating the pretty façade of the house. She caught his wicked grin, and then he was ushering her inside.

The reception-room was simply but elegantly furnished, its walls roughly plastered in Elizabethan style, its ceiling low and timbered with massive oak beams. Several paintings of horses hung on the walls, some of them evidently eighteenth-century, and obviously very valuable. A pair of fencing foils were crossed on one wall, below a rack of shotguns.

The stone inglenook fireplace was big enough to accommodate a roasting ox. Now it held a Scandinavian wood-burning stove decorated with cast polar bears, and Adam set a match to the pile of logs inside it. As the flames leaped eagerly along the kindling, he rose to study her. She was still gaping around her, her heart thudding heavily against her ribs. Where were the medics, the nurses, the clinic, the clean white corridors of her imagining?

The need surged in her, making her start shivering again. The Methadone was wearing off slightly now. She felt as though she were losing her buoyancy, beginning to sink in cold water.

'Give me your coat.'

She didn't resist as he helped her off with her coat. He was very tall, taller than she'd remembered. The grey eyes that looked down on her were penetrating, assessing. She flinched as he brushed the dark hair away from her temples.

'A pity,' he said softly. 'You would be so beautiful if you didn't look so ill.'

As she stared up into his face, Margot felt that there was something alien, remote about Adam Korda. Something that belonged to mountains, deserts, high and savage places. Had she been taken captive by a fanatic, a dangerous and unbalanced man? Fear twisted her stomach.

Tears were suddenly dangerously close, and she had to fight them down. 'What are you going to do to me?' she asked jerkily. 'Where are the doctors? Where are the staff? Why isn't there anyone else here? I need another pill! I have to have something, now!'

'No.'

The calm refusal was like a slap in the face. 'Why not?' she demanded angrily.

'Because Methadone's addictive.'

'That's not a very funny joke,' she snapped. 'I thought you were supposed to be helping me?'

Her imperious tone didn't move Adam in the slightest. 'It isn't a joke. And I am helping you.' His mouth was deeply, sensuously carved. But there was no softness in it. 'God knows you're incapable of helping yourself.'

'Just one more,' she pleaded. Reality was flooding in now, and with it pain and fear. She didn't bother to try and lie about how dependent she'd become on the white powder, now. Neither to him, nor to herself.

Odd, she thought with a remote, cold corner of her mind. When you'd taken the stuff, you were sure you could do without it. It was only when it started wearing off that you knew you couldn't. She opened dry lips. 'One more Methadone. *Please.*' She tried to sound adult, in control of herself. 'I need something, now.'

'You're going to have to stop thinking about drugs,' he said, his denial not unfriendly, just unmoved. 'And you're going to have to start facing up to a life without them.'

She felt the nerveways tightening all along her body, slowly, inexorably. Twelve hours without heroin. Margot sank into the sofa behind her, her hands trembling as she hugged herself. 'Listen,' she said shakily, 'you can't keep me here very long. No matter what you want to do. You *can't*.' She swallowed painfully. 'You've got to understand—I—I need something. Soon.'

'Finished? Then I'll make some coffee,' he said calmly, turning to go.

'Wait!' She took a slow breath, afraid of her wildly beating heart. She had to stay calm. Some primitive instinct was telling her not to show fear. 'OK, maybe you're right. Maybe I've got a problem, but it isn't the sort of problem you'll be able to cope with. I need to see a doctor.'

'There's a doctor within a few minutes' call, if necessary.' He considered her with one fist on his hip, eyes hooded. The soft light threw pools of shadow under his broad cheekbones and angular jaw. 'But I don't think we'll be needing her. Not yet, at any rate.'

'*Damn you!*'

'Don't scream at me.' The descending curve of his dark brows stemmed her rising hysteria. 'You're going to have to grow up, Margot. Fast.' He walked to the window, drew the curtains. She sat in nightmarish paralysis. If only she hadn't stepped into the Mercedes that morning, if only she had that split second of lost time again——

'You're right, though. You're going to start being sick,' he said flatly, turning to her. Dark eyelashes emphasised the shock of that grey stare. He wasn't smiling now. 'But not as sick as you imagine. Addicts greatly exaggerate the severity of withdrawal symptoms. Most people do, especially the dealers.'

'How the hell would you know?' Margot demanded with another flash of anger. Her face held an almost transparent beauty, her eyes large and feverish as they stared up at him. 'You talk like some kind of oracle!'

'There are various ways of making it easier,' he said, unperturbed by her glare. 'None of them are completely without some kind of risk, either of further addiction, or of damage to health.' He lifted one of the fencing foils from the wall. The needle point glinted as he sighted down the sword at her, eyes narrowed. 'In your case, I think a complete withdrawal is appropriate.'

It was only then that she began to understand him.

Realisation was like a jolt of electricity, it hurt and terrified.

'Oh no,' she whispered. 'You're going to make me go through cold turkey, aren't you? You're going to just sit there and watch me go through hell!'

CHAPTER TWO

'I WOULDN'T have put it so melodramatically,' he smiled. 'But in essence, the answer is yes.'

'You *can't*!'

'Oh, I can and will,' he promised her with cool certainty.

'B-but that's monstrous!'

'I thought you weren't an addict?'

'I said I might have a problem, damn you!' Margot's whole body was shaking now, panic sending the adrenalin surging into her bloodstream. 'Is that what you want? To hear me admit that I'm hooked?'

'That would make a good start,' he nodded.

'All right!' she said desperately. 'Maybe I *am* hooked! But you can't make me stop this way—I'll die!'

'You won't.' He curved the thin blade of the foil into a taut arc, the deeply incised lines tightening around his mouth. 'That's child's talk. No one dies of giving up heroin, I assure you. It's staying on the drug that kills. Coming off it is no worse than a severe bout of 'flu.'

'You don't know what you're talking about,' she said shakily, praying that he didn't mean it.

Cold turkey. Complete and abrupt withdrawal from drugs, with nothing to keep away the agony. He couldn't do it to her, he couldn't!

But she knew instinctively that he was not a man to say things idly. He wouldn't have got her all this way if he hadn't had the conviction to make her do as he said.

Adam laid the foil back on its rack and pulled off his jacket and tie, tossing them on to the armchair. 'Let me explain it to you, pearl. You and I are going to be spending the next fortnight here. Together.' She stared at him in horror as he came to sit beside her. At the V of his shirt, the muscular flesh was deeply tanned. 'You're not going anywhere,' he said in a velvety voice, 'not tonight, not any time. Everything is being taken care of. The rent on your flat in London is being paid. Your car has been safely garaged. People will hardly notice you're gone. And you're not leaving here until you're completely free of your addiction. Apart from that,' he smiled, showing beautiful white teeth, 'you're quite free to do anything you want. Roll your sleeve up.'

'What for?' she asked in dread.

'I want to check your blood pressure.'

She obeyed, claustrophobia hemming her in. She was as much in his power as a mouse between a cat's claws. 'Please don't think I won't go through with this, Margot,' he said conversationally. 'I fully intend to.' He pumped the bag up till it hurt, then slowly deflated it, eyes on the mercury level.

'You can't do this to me.' She was fighting to stem the rising tide of panic. 'You can't take the responsibility!'

'Oh, I can and I will,' he said with massive self-confidence. 'I take responsibility for other people's lives every day.'

'Are—are you a doctor?'

'No.' He unstrapped the bag. 'Your blood pressure's low, which is good. It's going to rise.'

'You're not a doctor! Then you don't know what will happen to me,' she pleaded.

He took her left hand, fingers biting into her wrist as he

timed her pulse. 'You've been using heroin for a mercifully short time. You've also smoked the poison, which is a great deal better than shooting it up.' He glanced at her. 'You're frightened. Your heart's racing. But it's steady enough.' He released her wrist. 'After three or four days you're going to be over the worst, Margot. Within a week or two you'll be feeling almost normal.'

Margot was feeling a sensation of coming down. The Methadone was definitely beginning to ebb out of her system now—the pains in her chest told her that. She was like a ship, foundering on rocks.

'It isn't necessary to do it like this,' she implored. Sweat was prickling at her temples and on her upper lip. 'I can stop any time I want to!'

'Can you?' he asked drily. 'Well, now's your chance to prove it.'

He didn't understand, she realised despairingly. She had to get away from him, it was her only chance. Wait for an opening, then run. Run back through the park to the road . . .

But they were out in the country now, she had no idea where, possibly very remote indeed. How far was it to the nearest town? He'd said there was a doctor close by, but she didn't know where. Despair told her she didn't have a hope in hell of finding help. He watched her expression with the cold eyes of a snow leopard, as though following every thought.

'Nobody will know where I am,' she quavered. 'People are going to worry——'

'I doubt it,' he said with brutal coldness. 'You don't have a job to go to. You left *City News* two months ago. They were afraid something like this would happen, weren't they?'

'How do you know——'

'Your mother hasn't seen you in weeks,' he went on brusquely. 'She doesn't even know you're an addict. Anyhow, you're going to telephone her tomorrow, and tell her you're taking a short break in Scotland. As for your friends——' He shrugged scornfully. 'I doubt whether you have the kind of friends who'll raise eyebrows at a brief disappearance—especially now that it's getting around you're a heroin user.' The cold grey eyes were painfully direct. 'It gets around very quickly, I'm afraid. Heroin attracts a lot of extremely nasty publicity.'

She tried to muster the strength to talk to him logically. 'I understand that you're concerned about the heroin,' she said, choosing her words with brittle care. 'You were a friend of my father's, and I know you think you can help me. But it isn't as simple as that.' She looked into the authoritative eyes. 'You have no right to do this, nothing on earth gives you the right. Can't you understand, I don't *know* you! I can't just put myself in your hands, like a child. I need someone I can trust——'

'You don't have anyone.' The words were spoken silkily, but they cut like a whip. 'You don't have a family, Margot, not any more. You don't have a lover. You don't have a friend strong enough to cope with this.' The deeply carved mouth smiled. 'And you don't have the will to give up on your own. You need someone. You need me.'

She sat in silence, eyes closed as if to shut out the world. *You need me.* Such frightening words.

Adam took her chin in strong fingers, making her open her eyes to face his stare. 'You understood how serious it all was, surely?' he demanded. 'Or did you want to let it kill you—suicide by narcosis?'

'Of course not——'

'If you don't give it up now, Margot, you just don't have a future.'

His words seemed to hang in the air, too chilling to warrant much in the way of a reply from her. In the velvety night outside an owl hooted, a lonely, wild cry.

She knew exactly how heroin could drag someone down to the abject death of the long-term addict. She'd seen it happen perhaps a dozen times since she'd left *City News* to enter the strange, twilight world of the drugs scene. The past weeks had been a kind of madness she knew had to end. But to do it this way, under the compulsion of a stranger——

She was as cold as ice again, her skin clammy and crawling with nerves.

'Three more questions,' he said. 'Are you on any other drugs apart from heroin?'

She shook her head without speaking. This couldn't be happening, couldn't be. There had to be some way out, there had always been a way out before. Something she could offer him, some bribe to let her go . . .

'No amphetamines, no barbiturates?'

'No,' she said in a low voice.

'Don't lie to me,' he said grimly. 'Heroin is one of the drugs you *can* just come off. Pills can be a lot more complicated.'

'I've never taken them.'

'And you've never injected heroin?'

She grimaced. 'No.'

'Good.' His eyes dropped to her lap. 'You're not pregnant, are you?'

'What the hell has *that* got to do with you?' she snapped angrily.

'It's got more to do with your unborn baby—if you're carrying one.' He smiled without humour. 'Because the foetus will be an addict. Like you. But, unlike you, it might not survive the withdrawal syndrome.'

Margot stared at him in horror. The words had shocked her more than anything else in the past hours. And for the first time she had an inkling of how this man must despise her, of how unlovely she must seem to him ...

'I'm not pregnant,' she said in a small voice.

'How much heroin were you using by last night?'

Margot's mouth trembled. 'I—I don't know.'

'Yes, you do,' came the quiet answer. 'Twice as much as when you started, I'd guess. A gram a day?'

'Not as much as that.' She swallowed, her throat dry as cardboard. 'Half that.'

'Are you telling the truth?' There was a dangerous edge beneath the soft voice. She nodded silently. 'Good. It could have been worse.' He took her chin, tilting her face up so that she had to meet the eyes that were the colour of an Arctic fjord. 'You know how potent heroin is. Deep down inside, you know that you're already an addict. You were an addict from the first moment you took the stuff. That means you're going to get withdrawal symptoms as bad as any long-term user's. There's no remission for only having used it a short while. Understand?'

'Yes,' she whispered. With odd clarity she noticed that there was a fine stubble round his lips and cheeks, that the muscles under his silk shirt were sleek and hard.

'You're also going to lose your tolerance very quickly, Margot. Try the stuff again, and you'll maybe kill yourself. Understood?'

'Yes.' She could hardly form the word. She knew

addicts could die using heroin half-way through
detoxification.

The thought underlined the frighteningly vulnerable
position she was in. For the first time she was realising that
every second was putting her more and more in this man's
power. As she entered the darkness of withdrawal, she was
going to need someone there, even a stranger she couldn't
trust. She was going to lose any control over her life. What
he'd said was going to become true, inevitably. She was
going to need Adam. Utterly.

He'd forced her to take the first steps along a path that
led into a wilderness. A path on which there could be no
turning back.

She felt the first spasms in her stomach. 'Where's the
bathroom?' she asked in a choked voice. 'I'm going to be
sick.'

He held her forehead while she was sick, making her feel
like a feverish child. When she was done, he leaned against
the wall, waiting while she rinsed her face with trembling
hands.

'Now I'll show you where your bedroom is,' he said
gently as she dried herself.

'My bedroom . . .?' She was almost too stunned to think.

The beautifully furnished room might have been
designed exclusively for her. Curtains, quilt and lamp-
shades were in a delicate patterned chintz, the simple yet
elegant furniture was of just the sort she liked most. Even
the colours were her favourites. An ivory-white room.
Ivory-white, for a maiden's tower.

Margot sat on the bed, fingers digging into the soft
quilt. 'How long have you been planning all this?' she
asked tautly.

'Not very long,' Adam shrugged. 'I didn't have a great deal of time. Which reminds me.' He opened the cupboard door. 'I bought a few clothes, but I had to guess your size. Not everything will fit.'

Margot stared dully at the row of skirts hanging on the rail, the gleam of silk in the drawers. He'd been choosing these pretty clothes for her, planning her abduction ... The room was warm, and her skin was damp with perspiration, yet her body was cold to the core.

'When are you going to let me go?' she asked quietly.

'I told you. When you're better.' He smiled at her with a hint of mockery, as though her suffering meant nothing to him. His dark face was magnificently handsome. 'You've been a little idiot, Margot. Now you're going to have to face up to yourself.'

'I can't do it.' She shook her head dumbly, not looking up. Desire for the drug was like a raging thirst. She'd never known she could want it so much. 'I *can't*!'

'You have to.' He poured her a glass of Perrier water from the bottle next to her bed. 'This might help with the nausea.' She lifted the rim of the glass to her lips, drinking a little with a wince of pain. His expression was still a mixture of amusement and assessment. 'Your father warned me that you were full of character. Perhaps you're more like him than you know.'

Margot shot him a spiteful glance. 'You seem to think that being Daddy's friend gives you an automatic right to interfere with my life. It doesn't, *Mr* Korda. I hardly knew my father. I didn't owe him a damned thing!'

'Owe?' he said with a glitter in his eyes that might have been anger. 'That's a funny way of putting it.'

She snorted. 'Having your parents break up when you're five years old isn't exactly reassuring,' she said shortly. 'Having them do it again when you're fifteen tends to make you think they've got something against you.'

'My, my,' Adam purred. 'I wonder how you get around at all, with that enormous chip on your shoulder.'

'Oh, go to hell! Daddy was totally irresponsible, and you know it. I knew him for two years during a very confused adolescence. Besides that, I saw him maybe half a dozen times in my *life*.' She leaned back against the pillows, every line of her slender body taut as a dancer's. 'Sometimes whole years would go by and I wouldn't see him. Don't expect me to forgive what you're doing to me—for Daddy's sake.'

Adam's eyes drifted across the angle of her hips, the slim length of her thighs. 'I don't want your forgiveness,' he said coolly. 'And talking of responsibility, you've hardly been an angel yourself, have you? Heroin is only the latest in the long line of Margot Prescott's delinquencies.'

'That's not true!'

'Oh, come on,' he mocked. 'You've been arrested twice, girl. Once for being accessory to stealing a car and the second time you were lucky not to be jailed, when you were picked up during a demonstration outside——'

'That happened to be something I felt very strongly about,' she snapped angrily. 'And the police behaved like fascists!'

'Using abusive language and resisting arrest, wasn't it?' He laughed huskily, warm golden flecks dancing in his eyes. 'You're quite a spitfire, Miss Prescott. It seems a pity to quench all that anger with heroin.'

She looked wearily up at him, so tall and arrogant in his power. She was nineteen. He was perhaps thirty-two or three. He'd never be able to understand a thing about her . . .

'How do you know all this?' Margot asked tiredly. 'Did my father tell you?'

'Most if it,' he nodded. 'I spoke to lots of people about you, though. You'd be surprised how many people care a great deal about you, *chérie.*'

'Would I?' she challenged drily. 'But then it's such a loving, caring world.'

'You're a strange child,' said Adam in a cool voice. 'I can't decide whether you're the most cynical little brat I've ever met——'

'Or?' she challenged as he paused.

'Or practically crippled with insecurity.'

Margot twisted on to her side, hugging the pillows to her face. Bastard. He knew a damned sight too much about her. He knew exactly where and how to hurt. God, if only she had something to take, something to shut out the pain that was building up in her nerves. She squeezed her eyes shut against the tears that had started to well up, but they found their way through her long, dark lashes nevertheless.

'It's past midnight,' Adam said quietly. 'You should try to sleep.' She didn't resist as he pulled the quilt around her shoulders. Adam had beautiful hands, she noticed absently, strong and capable, like everything about him. He lifted a hand now to touch her cold cheek with warm fingers. 'A woman shouldn't hate her father, even if he was irresponsible.'

Margot turned her face away from his touch. 'What did you owe my father?' she asked in a choked voice. 'Money? A favour?' She wiped her cheek with shaky fingers. 'Or are you doing this out of guilt?'

'Nasty,' he purred with soft amusement. 'I'm doing it for your sake, Margot.' She felt his lips touch her cheek warmly. 'We'll talk about it tomorrow. We've got all the time in the world. Try and sleep, pearl. My room is just next door to yours. If you want anything, anything at all, call me.'

She didn't respond, and heard her door close softly.

The silence was immense. Her digs in London had been so noisy at night, the incessant hum of traffic going on right through the night. She was shivering again, and there seemed to be no way she could get warm. Best not to think about her body. Best to think about something else, anything . . .

She clambered stiffly out of bed. The window was locked. Of course. Outside, the silvery moon shone down on dense, rustling woodland. Damn him.

She flung open the cupboard. There were cream silk pyjamas in the drawer, lacy and feminine. With a twisted smile, she started undressing. Her body was as tight as a coiled spring, waiting to explode, but the silk was cool and soothing on her bare skin.

She'd been in some strange places in her short life, but this was the strangest of them all, she reflected, getting back into bed.

Her father's friend. For all she knew, Adam Korda was a mercenary, as Peter had been, a hired killer with some twisted code of ethics that was better suited to the jungle than to the complex world of urban England . . .

She let herself drift for a long while, her mind full of cloudy memories of her father.

Peter Prescott had been a brilliant man with a wilful, erratic personality. His career in the Army had been outstanding, yet always poised on a knife-edge between originality and outright rebellion.

The same, Margot now understood, had applied to everything in his life—including his marriage to her mother. Margot had been born into a marriage that was already breaking up. Her very first memories were of childish terror at the arguments her parents used to have every night.

She'd been five years old when her father had finally made the break. Major Prescott had left his wife and child, and the Army, to assist in an African revolution. To become a mercenary.

Margot had been devastated. All her troubles had really begun at this point, although it had not been until much later that they'd flared up.

She hadn't seen her father for the next eight years, although he'd written, and now and then a birthday present had arrived from some remote corner of the globe. In that time, Margot's life had been touched with that desperate attempt at normality which so many children of broken homes know. Eleanor, her mother, had taken two consecutive lovers. With a child's innocence, Margot had called both men Daddy, but in her heart she'd always known that they weren't.

But when Margot was thirteen, and entering a slightly late puberty, Peter had returned to try and patch up his marriage with Eleanor.

Even now, a slow smile curled across her full mouth at the memory of that joy. God! She'd been so happy to have her father back ... It was the answer to a thousand dreams.

But six months turned it all sour. The arguments had been renewed, with even more savagery than eight years ago. And with the return of the quarrelling, Margot had known a dread that had only grown while it had been buried for those eight years.

It was then that her wilfulness and disobedience had flared up, at the worst possible time for all of them. Like drinking and breaking other people's windows. And worse. Almost as though she deliberately wanted to make their lives even more hellish.

Oh, Peter and Eleanor had grown miles apart in the intervening years, and that had made their prospects of compromise almost non-existent. But Margot knew, deep inside, that her own wildness had helped destroy whatever chance her parents' marriage had ever had.

Two years later, before Margot's fifteenth birthday, it was all over. Peter had left England again to become military advisor to a Gulf State prince. He'd barely said goodbye to her before he'd left. 'England's finished for me. Goodbye, Margot, good luck, darling.'

That was all.

Her dominant emotion at the time had been disbelief. *This can't be happening again.* But it was happening, and this time with a finality she couldn't avoid. After that, no one and nothing seemed to matter to Margot. Even when her mother had remarried, and in her late thirties had given birth to two more children to her new husband, Margot had watched with an unmoved, cynical smile.

And the company she'd started to choose had supported her in her hardening attitudes. She'd joined the lunatic fringe of the anti-war movement—a direct hit at her father—had moved in a circle of friends who were often little better than criminals. Rebels against authority, or what they bitterly called 'The Establishment'. Pranks had turned into deliberate destruction . . .

She'd slipped from delinquency into a wildness that was

too much for her mother to handle.

Her stepfather, Carl Davison, had been only too pleased when Margot had left home to live in digs. And for the past three and a half years, since her sixteenth birthday. Margot had gone her own way.

She rolled restlessly over on to her left side, hugging her shivering shoulders, and stared ahead with unseeing, dark eyes for a long while.

The thought of the coming hours filled her with fear. This wasn't the place for her. Adam with the grey eyes was a nightmare she had to awaken from. If she had to give up heroin, she would do it her own way. Not on anyone else's terms.

But she'd never known an addict who'd given up heroin. Even Riff, who had first given her the drug, had never been able to kick it.

Clever Riff. He'd always been so intent on pushing the stuff, so intent on the money he was making out of it. Riff's business was making sure other people got addicted and stayed that way. And yet the drug had had him as surely in its grip as any of his customers. Except that Riff was now in jail, and likely to stay there a long time.

To kill yourself with heroin. She shook the thoughts away, She needed to sleep, regain her strength. Tomorrow she was going to be feeling terrible, and she would most need her strength. Tomorrow she would get out of here, whatever it took. Back to London, somehow, anyhow.

An owl hooted again, in the vast night. She reached out with unsteady fingers to switch off the light, and tried to sleep.

She was sick several times throughout the night, her insides feeling as if they were being turned inside out. But somehow, in between bouts, she managed to slip gratefully into a restless sleep.

Since she'd been on heroin, her sleep had been dreamless and dead. But tonight nightmares came, a confused incubus of terror that went on and on. A faceless horror, pursuing her down endless corridors, carrying a glittering syringe that she knew was filled with her death. Until she was trapped in a corner, and the deadly point was thrusting at her naked throat——

She awoke in panic, her heart pounding furiously. Strong hands were grasping her shoulders, and she realised that Adam was sitting on her bed, calling her name.

'Margot, it's all right. Take it easy.'

'My heart . . .' Her chest was constricted by iron bands. She'd never felt her pulses beat so wildly in her life, and it terrified her. 'My heart,' she gasped again. 'I think I'm going to have a heart attack!'

He laid his warm palm across the clammy, cold skin of her breast, feeling for the beating heart beneath. 'Fast,' he nodded, 'but not serious. You can expect this to happen, especially at first. It's not dangerous.' She felt his hand touch her damp forehead. 'Try and breathe deeply and steadily. That will slow it down.'

She obeyed, her body trembling like a trapped bird's. In the soft darkness she could see he was naked to the waist, the moonlight gleaming on his skin. He was powerfully built, a dark shadow of masculine hair covering his chest and stomach.

'Any better?' he asked.

'A little,' she panted. She realised that her fingers were still clawing into his muscular arm, as if seeking comfort.

A little ashamedly, she released her grip. 'S-sorry. Did I scratch you?'

'I'll live.' He brushed the damp hair away from her brow. 'It must have been a bad nightmare.'

'Horrible,' she whimpered.

'You've got a lot of dreaming to catch up on, pearl.' The dark made his husky voice seem warm and intimate. The very closeness of him was comforting. 'Heroin has stopped you dreaming for a long time. But the dreams didn't just go away. They've built up, and now they're all going to come rushing back.'

'I don't want to have any more nightmares,' she pleaded.

'Do you want me to put the light on?'

'No,' she shivered. Her heartbeat was easing now. 'Was I screaming my head off?'

'You were sort of squeaking,' he smiled. 'Like a kitten.' Before she understood what he was doing, he had pulled the quilt aside, and was sliding into the bed beside her. 'It's damned cold, pearl. Move over.'

She stiffened in a moment of panic, then tried to back as far away from him as she could manage.

'Do you imagine I'm burning to make love to you?' he enquired drily. 'I'll try and restrain my lust. This'll just save me the walk after your next nightmare.'

She was still shivering uncontrollably, her heart racing. 'Just d-don't g-get any ideas,' she quavered.

'What sort of ideas?' he purred. She felt the brush of his warm skin against hers as he reached for her, pulling her close.

His near-naked body was so different from hers. Warm where hers was cold. Hard where hers was soft, potent where hers was delicate. His lips were firm and authoritative against hers, his kiss warm without being invasive. 'Do you expect me to lay a sword between us?' he said softly. 'You'll warm up now. You're as cold as clay.'

As the shock receded, she became aware of the length of his body against hers, the power of his arms around her, her hips against him. She could smell his skin, his hair, even feel the beating of his heart against her breasts. A world that was new to her, or at least so unfamiliar as to be new.

The fear slid away, her breathing easing. There was immense comfort in his embrace. Something she hadn't felt for years. Protection and warmth, a sense of wholeness. Slowly, she relaxed in his arms, the stiffness in her slender body melting by degrees.

'That's better,' Adam murmured softly. His face was close against her hair. 'You smell sweet, the way a woman should.' She felt his fingers trail down her back. 'What were you dreaming of?'

'N-nothing important.'

'Important enough to make you wake up screaming.'

'Confused things, I don't know . . . Someone chasing me . . . with a syringe. Trying to kill me.'

'A direct expression of your own fear of heroin,' Adam said unhesitatingly. 'Your unconscious mind screaming at you to save yourself.' His lips were so close to hers that she could feel his warm breath on her cheek. 'Are you feeling any better?'

'Yes,' she whispered.

'And getting used to the idea of a strange man in your bed?'

'Yes. No!'

'I like that. Yes, no.' The warm breath of his quiet laughter caressed her throat. 'A totally feminine response.

I don't think you've lain in bed with many men, pearl.'

'I'm not a child,' she retorted, her lips almost touching the satiny skin of his shoulder.

'Yes, you are,' he contradicted her. 'A child who does crazy things, like getting hooked on heroin. A child who gets nightmares, and has to be comforted.' He pillowed her head against his broad chest, and she closed her eyes, the smell of his skin warm and musky in her nostrils. Beneath her cheek, she could feel his heart pumping steadily and strongly.

It was so long since a man had held her like this . . .

'Go to sleep, pearl,' she heard his husky voice telling her. 'You won't have any more nightmares tonight, I promise.'

She lay in silence, intensely aware of his nakedness against her. Imperceptibly, unbidden, the possibility of their making love crept into her mind. Margot touched the thought with mental fingertips, exploring it, at first timidly, then with growing boldness. It could happen. If she let him, perhaps he would . . .

Suddenly, she wanted him. No sentiment, no words, she just wanted him to make love to her, with the complete power she knew he was capable of, obliterating every thought in her mind . . .

She felt the groaning ache of desire in her loins, and no shame or modesty would quench it. She could never ask him, never. The idea was horrifying, and yet the need was there.

Her feverish thoughts twisted restlessly. What did Adam Korda really think of her? Under that teasing, dry manner, he probably despised her utterly. He would never understand her, would never understand how she'd ended up on heroin. Although he was only a dozen or so years older than her, he came from a generation and a social class that was very remote from hers. Clearly wealthy and successful, he had that unmistakable stamp of authority. From where he stood, she was an amusing oddity, a crumpled failure with a wing down . . .

God, she was so lonely! Where was she going? What was going to happen to her? She clung to his quietly breathing body, the tears stealing past her shut lids, spilling on to his skin.

If he was aware of their wetness on his chest, he made no sign of it.

CHAPTER THREE

ADAM was gone by the time Margot woke. She sat up, feeling utterly wretched. Her head was throbbing like an engine as she ran her fingers through her tangled hair.

'A bad dose of 'flu.' Her eyes and nose were streaming, and there was an ominous rattle in her chest every time she breathed. The headache was frightful, picking up volume all the time. The bright autumn light from the window stabbed painfully into her eyes.

She clambered weakly out of the bed, found a dressing-gown behind the door, and made her way to the bathroom. She felt as though she were moving through thick fog.

Had she really slept beside Adam Korda all night?

She stumbled. Oh, *damn* . . . She was feeling even worse than she'd realised, the deep muscles of her limbs trembly and aching. Her empty stomach was knotting in cramps already.

Someone was in the bathroom already. A middle-aged woman in an apron was reeling up the cable of a vacuum cleaner. She turned to glance at Margot, and smiled.

'Hello, dear. Glad you're awake. How are you feeling?'

'Like death warmed over,' Margot said thickly, knowing she must look terrible. She clutched her gown around her. 'Where's Adam?'

'Mr Adam's up at the stables.' The country face was

pleasant. 'He's been with the horses since five this morning.'

'The stables.' Margo repeated stupidly.

'Aye. Up at the stud.'

'Is that what this place is? A stud farm? It really isn't a—an institution, then?'

'An institution? You mean a *mental* institution?' The older woman looked amused. 'Why, no. Whatever put that notion into your head? You're at Harcourt Hall, dear. One of the biggest stud farms in England.'

Margot swallowed as she took that in. 'Wh-when will he be back?'

'In about an hour, I think.'

Time enough for her to get a long way from this jail! If only she had the strength . . . 'How—how far are we from London?'

She frowned. 'I don't think I could say, exactly. We generally go on the coach. But you don't want to be worrying about things like *that*. I've got your breakfast on the go.' She bustled past Margot. 'There's plenty of hot water, and I've laid fresh towels out for you. You should have everything you need. Your clothes are still in the wash, of course, but I expect you've been told there are new things in your room.'

'Wait,' Margot pleaded. 'Do you know who I am?'

'Miss Prescott, from London.' The woman smiled. 'I'm forgetting my manners. My name's Aileen Bell. My husband, George, works up at the stud, and I do a bit of housework for Mr Adam.'

'Mrs Bell, you've got to help me,' Margot said urgently.

'Anything you want,' Aileen Bell replied pleasantly.

'I'd like to leave here this morning. I *have* to leave here.

That coach you mentioned—where does it start from?'

'The village,' the middle-aged woman said promptly. 'But that's four miles away, and it only goes on Tuesdays and Thursdays. Have your bath, dear, and by the time you're finished I'll have your breakfast ready.'

'But I have to go,' said Margot with the nervous energy of a cornered animal. 'I'm not here of my own will!'

'You don't have to tell me that,' the housekeeper replied gently. Lined eyes assessed Margot's pale face and shaky hands. 'But I know enough about you to know that you're here for your own good. What you need is plenty of country air—and plenty of good country food.'

'*Please*——'

'You'll feel a hundred times better after your bath.'

Hopelessly, Margot let herself be pushed into the white-tiled bathroom. Trust Adam to have employed the village idiot! Damn him to hell for his meddling, interfering *arrogance*——

She sat on the edge of the bath and wept silently, as much from the pain in her stomach and abdomen as from frustration. She was as weak and helpless as a child.

God, what she wouldn't give for a painkiller, even a miserable aspirin! She recalled Adam scattering the precious white powder on the grass, and moaned . . .

After a few minutes, she dragged herself into the shower, and stood passively under the stingingly hot needles of water.

In the steamy confines of the cubicle she had a paroxysm of sneezing, and half-way through lathering her hair, she had to double over, retching in futile spasms.

In a kind of weak fury, Margot emerged from the shower, and started towelling herself dry. She was going to get herself out of here today, she swore it grimly. Away from this indignity and suffering. She'd hitch a lift to the village, wherever it was. There were still a few hundred pounds in her bank account, the last of her savings from the *City News* days. She'd find a branch, draw enough money to get that coach back to London. She'd do it, somehow, even if it meant stabbing *Mr* Adam with one of the fencing foils off the wall.

In the full-length mirror, her body was pale and very slender. In the summer she'd been tanned, carrying at least an extra stone. Such a long, long time ago.

People who take heroin don't dream . . .

She framed herself with the outspread towel, staring at her own image. A dark cloud of hair surrounding an oval face whose beauty was somehow fragile. It was only a certain wilful look in her dark eyes and a passionate slant to her wide mouth which hinted at her inner strength.

The cheekbones, emphasised by her slimness, were exquisite, as was the column of her throat and the delicate wings of her collarbones. Her breasts were full without heaviness, taut and feminine. Men had always admired her, desired her long, dancer's legs, told her that her hands and face were lovely; yet she'd never been able to quite believe it, not deep down. There was always that feeling, deep inside, that she was ugly. That no man could ever love or desire her enough to stay.

Not for ever.

She sat at the mirror, feeling as though a steel spring was coiling up inside her. As Mrs Bell had promised, everything had been laid out for a very fussy woman. The temptations to smash the alluring bottles against the mirror was overwhelming for a moment. Then it slid away.

Listlessly, she opened a pot of face cream. One of those prohibitively expensive pseudo-scientific formulas. Mr Adam must be used to women with costly tastes. Rubbing it into her skin, she saw that there were dark shadows under her eyes. Her skin had lost the pearly glow of health, too. It was lifeless and dry-looking, her lips cracked and neglected. She looked sick, and felt worse.

She was nervy and brittle as she hunted through the drawers, tossing the things she didn't want on to the floor. Let someone else pick them up. In half an hour she was going to be on the road home.

She found a beautiful white angora sweater, and a pair of charcoal jeans that fitted her. The underwear was all black silk, plain but elegant. There was also a pair of soft leather boots, not unlike ones she had in London.

But there was no sign of the money that had been in her clothes of yesterday.

How the *hell* was she going to get back to London without money? Nervous waves of anger were rippling inside her as she walked to the kitchen, jerking the fluffy sweater down over her compact hips. The smell of coffee and bacon was nauseating. Mrs Bell was just setting a tray, but Margot was tight-lipped and hostile.

'Where's my money?' she demanded unsteadily. 'The money that was in my clothes. Where is it?'

'It's safe and sound, dear,' the housekeeper said soothingly. 'You don't need it here——'

'Give it to me!'

'I'm sorry, honey.' The friendly eyes were genuinely regretful. 'Mr Adam left strict instructions that you weren't to have any money.'

'You're a thief,' Margot said savagely. 'And your master's a kidnapper!'

'Why, come to that, you might be right on both counts,' the other woman said with a smile, as though the idea had just occurred to her. 'Why not have your breakfast by the fire in the living-room? There's a lovely view over the park.'

She lifted the tray, on which was a plate of bacon and field mushrooms, and a bubbling percolator of fresh coffee, and offered it to Margot. Nausea rose in her, tightening her throat. Damn them all! With a sob of uncontrolled fury, she snatched the tray away, and hurled it across the kitchen.

The contents of the tray crashed noisily on to the floor, and Mrs Bell let out a little cry of anguish.

'Why, no! You didn't have to do that, girl!' Stiffly, she knelt by the mess, mourning over the smashed crockery as she picked up the pieces.

Adam's deep voice cut through the tense silence.

'Leave it, Aileen. I'll clear it up.' He was standing in the doorway, tall and grim. The clothes he wore were rough; hands thrust into the pockets of a heavy sheepskin jacket, legs long and muscular in faded jeans and riding boots. If only he'd been here a second ago, so she could have thrown the tray at him instead!

He glanced briefly at Margot's quivering expression, then helped the housekeeper to her feet. 'Miss Prescott's not feeling herself this morning,' he said quietly. 'I should have waited until she woke up. You'd better leave us together for the rest of the day.'

'I think I'd better.' The woman was obviously upset. She

didn't look at Margot as she dropped some broken crocks into the bin. 'I hope you know what you've taken on,' she remarked meaningfully.

'I've learned how to duck by this stage of my life,' he said drily. 'She didn't mean it. She'll apologise when she feels better.' Margot's legs were too weak to support her any longer. She sat at the kitchen table, burying her face in her hands, barely aware that Adam was showing Mrs Bell out of the cottage. She needed heroin, now. Nothing else would stop the frightened shaking and the stomach pains that were like the worst cramps she'd ever had.

She heard a small car driving away, then his step at the threshold. A strong hand took her arm, hauling her to her feet with effortless power. His eyes had an animal directness; with sharp clarity she remembered the eyes of a wolf she'd once seen in Amsterdam zoo, which had held the same crystalline, cold beauty. 'You didn't have to take it out on Aileen,' he rasped. 'She doesn't deserve your tantrums.'

Margot looked blindly up at him. 'What are you doing this for?' she choked. 'Why couldn't you have left me alone?'

'Because you're such a deserving case,' he said drily. 'I take it you're not feeling too hot?'

'It hurts so badly,' she moaned. 'I want an aspirin. Please. Anything!'

'I want, I need, I must have, I can't do without——' The scorn in his voice was scalding. 'All you do is demand things. Have you no resources of your own?'

'It isn't a crime to ask for a painkiller!' She pressed her fingers into her aching temples. 'You want me to suffer, is that it? Make wicked Margot learn her lesson?'

'You're going to telephone your mother now,' he said imperturbably. 'You're going to tell her you're taking a fortnight's holiday with friends. Give her this number, if she asks.' He scribbled a number on a piece of paper, then lifted the telephone off the wall, and held it out to her. She felt as though she were drowning in that compelling gaze. 'You can say whatever you please, pearl. But if you're considering any melodramatic rubbish, think twice. The whole story will have to come out. Your mother still doesn't know about you. You may not have much of a relationship with her, but I don't think you want her to know that you're a heroin addict. Do you?'

Margot took the telephone numbly. He was damnably right, as ever. She'd do a great deal to keep her mother from knowing. But the way she felt right now was frightening . . .

She dialled her mother's number shakily. Should she blurt out a plea for help, try and get a message through? As she listened to the ringing at the other end, her heart was pounding with indecision.

But it was her stepfather's voice which answered, and her shoulders slumped slightly. She'd never been able to ask him for anything in her life, and she couldn't start now.

'C-Carl?' she said dully. 'It's Margot. Is Mum there?'

'She's out,' he said without warmth. 'What is it, Margot?'

'I just . . . I just wanted to tell her I'm in Scotland.' She met Adam's merciless eyes, felt the compulsion in them. 'On holiday. With friends.'

'Yes?' Carl Davison prompted impatiently.

'Probably won't be back for a couple—a couple of

weeks.' She read him the number. 'Ask her if she'll ring me when she gets the chance,' she put in quickly. *'Please.'*

'I'll tell her,' said Carl without enthusiasm. 'Need any money or anything?'

For a flickering moment she debated whether to blurt out the truth, and then it passed. 'N-no. I'm fine.'

'Right. Anything else?'

'No,' she said in a small voice.

Carl Davison's goodbye was almost insultingly prompt. As the line was cut off in her ear, she sagged back miserably.

'He doesn't seem too keen on you,' Adam suggested, replacing the receiver for her.

'I don't get on with my stepfather,' she replied shortly. 'He thinks I'm a disruptive influence.'

'Which is just about right.' Adam considered her. 'You were wise not to say anything foolish, Margot. Kick as you may, this is probably the only chance you're ever going to get to save yourself.'

'Locking me up and making me go through cold turkey?' she said ironically. 'It's a rather simplistic approach, surely!'

'Maybe,' he nodded. 'If I felt you were an emotional cripple, and that your addiction was due to some underlying weakness of character, I would never have done it. But I don't think that.' There were gold flecks in his eyes, a hint of warmth in that Arctic cold. 'I think your addiction was some kind of accident, something that should never have happened. Come on. You need some fresh air.' He hauled a thick woollen fisherman's jersey off a hook behind the door and tossed it at her. 'Put that on, though. It's cold outside.'

Rebelliously, she pulled it on. It was several sizes too big, and she looked lost in it, almost waiflike. He grinned at her expression, but if there was sympathy in the wolf's eyes, it wasn't showing much. 'It's a beautiful autumn day. Let's go.'

Ignoring her resistance, he got her outside and into the chill, pure air.

The scenery was magnificent, she could see that even through her misery. The cottage was set half-way up a hill, in the heart of a great wood. October had flooded the leaves with an almost intoxicating range of scarlets and yellows, and each tree had its own palette of colour, beeches, maples, oaks, the occasional dark green spire of a conifer.

Below, the wood stretched down into the valley, and almost to the violet hills in the far distance. The nearest habitation she could see was a farmhouse several miles distant, the white smoke of its chimneys rising into the still air.

'This is Darkrising Wood,' Adam told her, eyes almost dreamy as he watched her face. 'It's thirteen centuries old. Like it?'

'Marvellous,' she said sullenly. 'So much to see and do. If you happen to be a squirrel. That woman said something about a stud farm. Does it belong to you?'

'Yes. I breed racehorses.' He looped a woollen scarf round her neck. His voice roughened slightly as he studied her unhappy face. 'For God's sake! Have you forgotten how to smile, Margot? You look as though someone's sewn your cheeks together from the inside.'

'I'm afraid I'm not one of your brood mares,' she

snapped, her head aching. 'I can't change my mood to order.'

'I wouldn't dream of breeding from you,' he retorted cuttingly. His eyes raked her slim figure. 'You may have the lines, but you don't have the temperament.' He more or less marched her across the path, and into Darkrising Wood. 'I want you to know something, Margot,' Adam went on levelly. 'I had a very dear brother, a year younger than me, who became a heroin addict. He was hooked more deeply than you, far more deeply than you can imagine. He kicked it, though. I was with him while he went through what you're experiencing now. It's not exactly new to me.'

'Did you have to kidnap him, too?' she asked harshly.

'No. He came off it voluntarily.'

'And what happened to him?' she demanded, curious despite herself.

His expression didn't change. 'He's dead now.'

'Oh, *great*.' A gust of wind sent her long, raven hair tumbling around her face. Her eyes were feverishly bright. 'A brilliant success. Is that the way I'm supposed to go?'

Adam glanced at her, the smile more in his eyes than his mouth. 'It wasn't coming off the heroin that killed him. It was something else.'

She snorted unsympathetically, not interested in anyone's suffering except her own. Within a few minutes they were far into the shadowy wood, ankle-deep in the rustling carpets of red and gold and brown. It was as silent as some great cathedral, barely a squirrel or a bird stirring in the still air.

And the beauty she'd been determined to ignore slowly

sank into her, bringing some peace. She rubbed her burning face, suddenly glad after all to be out of the cottage. 'I'm sorry,' she sighed at last. 'I didn't meant to sound flippant about your brother's death.'

'Forget it.' He moved with the unthinking grace of an animal, his body spare and supple and strong. She was ridiculously weak, and she felt him having to hold back his long strides so as not to tire her.

He would be good with horses, she thought instinctively. They would understand the male strength of those powerful thighs, the gentleness of those hands. Dominance and sensitivity, a rare combination.

'If you were a close friend of Daddy's,' she said, 'you must have lived abroad a lot. He was hardly ever in England.'

'Friendship doesn't necessarily depend on long periods spent in someone's company,' he said obliquely. 'If it's real, it goes on regardless of distance or time. For example, you were seldom out of your father's thoughts, even though you seldom saw each other. He talked about you a lot.'

'Did he?' she asked sceptically. 'What sort of things did he say?'

Adam glanced at her. 'He used to wonder whether you'd get over what he and your mother had done to you.'

'You never get over a broken home,' Margot said flatly. 'What else did he say about me?' she asked with a taut smile. 'That I helped break up the family, no doubt?'

'Why should anyone blame you for that?' he said, arching an eyebrow. 'It was a matter of two adults whose marriage didn't work.'

'I contributed,' she muttered.

He looked amused. 'How? By misbehaving? All

teenagers are difficult, Margot. It's hardly a crime.'

'I was more than difficult. I was crazy.' She kicked restlessly at the leaves underfoot, sending them rustling around her ankles. 'It seemed I couldn't do anything right. I was never out of trouble. If I hadn't been the way I was, they'd have had that much more time to work things out between themselves. In that way it was partly my fault, too ...'

The contact of his body was unexpected as his arm encircled her waist. She looked up into the warm challenge of his smiling mouth. 'Your fault, my fault, their fault—you're a great blamer, aren't you?' The support of that strong arm around her lower back somehow melted something inside her. 'Is that the world according to Margot Prescott? Everything everywhere is somebody's fault?'

'It just happens to be the way I feel,' she shrugged awkwardly. She met his eyes almost timidly. 'How—how did you find out about me? About the heroin, I mean?'

'I went to see you in London, about six weeks after Peter's death. I didn't have an address, just that you were working for *City News*. A woman there called Gillian Reynolds told me you'd resigned. She also told me she thought you'd become an addict.'

'I see.' Margot looked away, her cheeks flushing. Her journalistic career had been brief. She had submitted an angry article to an *avant-garde* newspaper called *City News*, when she'd been sixteen years old. They'd liked it and six months later she had joined the staff as a feebly paid but full-time junior reporter.

Somehow she'd survived the inevitable problems and difficulties of working for a rag that couldn't always meet its deadlines, and quite often couldn't pay its reporters.

Two years on, her career at *City News* was starting to show signs of brilliance. In those two years, *City News* had graduated from a trendy rag into a fashionable youth paper. And Margot Prescott had earned quite a reputation for hard-hitting investigative articles—with an anti-establishment bias, of course. And beautifully written, always. It was quite surprising how many of her stories had been syndicated to highly respected journals.

How long ago all that was, the heady moments of her success. The only time in her life that she'd felt she was achieving anything. Gill Reynolds had been her closest friend at *City News*, and she'd been one of those people who'd tried to throw her a lifebelt when she had first started using heroin. It hadn't helped; she'd already been too far in by then.

'What did you want to see me for?' she asked.

'I had some idea of offering my condolences,' Adam said gently. She was almost leaning on him now, weakness moulding her body to his side. 'Maybe trying to help. I felt it was a sort of obligation to your father. Whenever he talked about you he used to say the same thing: "I'll have to sort that girl of mine out one of these days."'

'But he never did,' said Margot in a low, dry voice, refusing to acknowledge that he'd touched a nerve. 'He got himself killed instead.'

'That's one thing you can't blame him for.' The husky warmth of his voice was almost like a caress, unexpectedly gentle from such a masculine man. 'It wasn't his fault that the plane crashed. But there was another reason I came to London, a purely selfish one.' His fingers curled even tighter around her slender waist as he smiled down at her.

'I wanted to meet you, because everything about you intrigued me. There was a certain contradictory fascination to Margot Prescott. Beautiful teenage rebel who'd become journalistic hot property. A totally unpredictable shooting star. Would she go up or down? No one had the faintest idea.'

'She went down,' Margot said with bitter irony. 'So you found a junkie. What made you decide on the big rescue act?' She was starting to run a fever, she could feel it now. She touched the damp skin of her temples with shaky fingers. 'There's more than just "obligation" behind all this. Isn't there?'

'Perhaps,' he said softly. 'Perhaps not. You're very hard on yourself, Margot.'

'What do you mean?' she demanded.

'I mean you seem to be convinced of your own worthlessness.' Was he mocking her or probing her psyche? She couldn't read his gentle smile. 'Do you know the difference between *shall* and *will*?' he asked.

'Haven't the faintest idea,' she muttered.

'Someone who's afraid they won't be rescued says, *I shall drown—no one will help me*. Someone who's determined to die says, *I will drown. No one shall help me*. Which one are you?'

'You're wasting your time, Adam.' She pulled away from him, and turned to face him with angry black eyes. 'Psychoanalysing me isn't going to help. I don't matter a damn to anybody, and nobody matters a damn to me. So why not just let me get back to my own life?'

'And let you go to hell your own way?' he challenged.

'If that's what I want, yes!'

'We're back to "I want", are we?' He faced her

aggressively, long legs spread, hands thrust into the pockets of his sheepskin jacket. 'You'll be twenty in a few months, Margot. When are you going to grow up?'

'Who says I'll ever reach twenty?' she sneered, more for effect than anything else. But the words made his handsome face tighten with real anger.

'Damn you!' Strong fingers knotted in her jersey, jerking her forward with a violence that made her teeth rap painfully in her head. His intensity was suddenly frightening, his strength so much vaster than hers. Her face was white as he glared into her eyes from a few inches away. 'Don't *ever* let me hear you speak like that again,' he said savagely. 'You're *not* worthless! You're precious, can't you understand that?'

'You're hurting me,' she whispered. 'And just who am I precious to?'

She saw his eyes glitter for a moment, as though he were assessing whether her words had been a challenge or a plea. Maybe she'd wanted him to kiss her then, she was too confused to tell. But she didn't draw back when he pulled her close.

She could only cling helplessly to his shoulders as firm, moist lips claimed her own. Adam's lean body was hard with muscle, his skin like hot silk, everything about him sensuous, a vividly male onslaught on her senses. His tongue slid with wicked expertise into her mouth, lean, strong arms crushing her against him as though he wanted to devour her.

The reaction of her body was electric, the hunger flaring along her arteries like a fuse, exploding into passion. Need for him was instantaneous and imperious, tightening the peaks of her breasts, meltingly sweet at her loins. She shuddered as he ran his fingers roughly through her dark hair, the tangles snagging cruelly, pressing his mouth to her throat.

His hands caressed across her ribs, cupping her breasts hungrily. She moaned in surrender as his thumbs brushed across the hardening points of her nipples, making her shudder helplessly, her mouth seeking his now, wanting to be bruised by the passion of his kiss.

Slowly, the onslaught receded. Her legs were unable to hold her when Adam released her, and she almost stumbled in weakness. She touched her mouth with shaky fingers; there was a smear of blood on her fingertips. Her blood.

'What did you do that for?' she whispered.

'I wish I knew,' he said tightly. She could almost sense the tension in him, see the flickering heat in his eyes as he stared down at her. She knew with trembling certainty that he was ready for her, ready to take her here, among the leaves. He drew a ragged breath. 'This isn't quite the way I planned your morning's breath of air.' He shook his head. 'Just remember that you're a beautiful, intelligent, gifted woman, Margot. It's time you started behaving and talking like one—and not like a backward adolescent.'

She stared at him with her lips parted, still stunned by that blazing kiss. She was trembling with shock, her womanhood aching for him unbearably.

'Come on.' Roughly, he pulled her back on to the track, his expression volatile. 'It's time we went home.'

At around five that evening, her mother called. Adam passed her the receiver expressionlessly, and she took it in both shaky hands.

'Mum! It's good to hear your voice!'

'That's an unexpected compliment,' her mother's cautious tones answered. 'Carl tells me you're on holiday in Scotland?'

'Yes. With—with some friends.'

'Having a nice time, I hope.'

Well,' she said with a wry smile, 'the weather's a bit unpredictable. Are you all right, Mum? How are the kids?'

'We're all fine,' her mother assured her. 'Just a bit worried about you. We never seem to hear from you these days. You must stay in touch, darling.'

'I'll try, I really will!'

'You sound a bit ragged,' Eleanor said in concern. 'Are you sure you're all right?'

Margot's eyes met Adam's. 'I've got—a rather bad cold, Mum,' she said, savouring the tiny inner joke. 'But they tell me it won't last long.'

'Well, take care of yourself, for goodness' sake. And come and see us when you get back from Scotland.'

'I will,' Margot promised. 'I don't know when that'll be, but I will.'

There was a muffled murmur, then her mother's voice came back on the line. 'Carl says, when are you going to start looking for another job? Anyway, don't bother about that now. Just have a good time.'

'I'll try, Margot said drily. 'I'll try.'

CHAPTER FOUR

ADAM laid the blanket around her shoulders. Margot clutched the soft wool with trembling fingers, looking up at him with eyes that screamed silently for help. She was close to the end of her tether.

It had been building up all day, and the sunset had brought on a peaking of the withdrawal symptoms. She was a bundle of taut, jangling nerves.

The moon was full, a golden disc in a velvet-blue sky. With the clarity of autumn, every star was bright as fire. She was huddled in the window-seat. Every fine hair on her arms was erect, her skin raised in the permanent gooseflesh that had such an ugly name.

Cold turkey.

She was trembling helplessly, and cold as ice despite the warmth of the fire. She had to fight down the sense of unbearable anxiety the whole time, grit her teeth against the tremors that shook her.

Mrs Bell had come to make a meal, and had gone again, but she'd been unable to eat a crumb, and Adam had hardly touched the food either.

Adam felt her pulse for half a minute, then squatted in front on her, his grey eyes narrow with concentration. 'This is the worst,' he said quietly. 'Stick it out, little one. It won't get any worse than this.'

'I don't know how——' Her voice stuck, and she tried again, shuddering. 'I don't know how long I can—stand this——'

'It won't last.' His eyes were so compelling. She tried to hold them with her own. There was a massive quality about him, something solid and hard that she could cling to in the raging storm of the drug leaving her system. 'Thank God we're nipping this in the bud. Another few weeks on heroin, and——' He broke off, capable hands arranging the hair away from her eyes. 'You'll need to drink plenty of liquids,' he went on. He'd brought a jug of fresh fruit juice, and he poured her a glass. 'Drink.'

The stuff was hateful, unacceptably acid in her mouth. She gulped it painfully down then gave him back the glass half-empty. 'I c-can't.'

'Just another sip. Please try.'

'Adam.' Her dark eyes were shiny with tears. 'Let me have another M-Methadone. I can't last through much more of it. P-Please, I'll never ask again . . .'

'Methadone is addictive,' he said with something close to compassion in his tanned face. 'It's just synthetic heroin.'

'I'm begging you,' she said abjectly.

'I can't simply give it to you.' He touched her cheek. 'It has to be administered in exact doses, in some controlled environment, like a hospital. Coming off heroin with Methadone will take three or four weeks, pearl. This way is better for you. By tomorrow, even, you'll be feeling better.' He touched her cold hands, smiling slightly. 'Remember that the symptoms are not in themselves dangerous. Most of your suffering is mental.'

Most of your suffering is mental.

'You superior bastard,' she said shakily, thrusting his hands away and getting up in a state of explosive tension. 'You talk so c-coldly and logically about it all. You think you can do what you please with me, pet me when you want to, punish me when you want to—as though I'm some kind of white mouse in an ex-experiment. I'm not! I'm a woman, Margot Prescott. This is happening to me!'

A convulsion of pain made her cry out, and she sank down on to her knees on the Persian rug, holding herself and crying jerkily with bowed head.

'I'm sorry.' His voice was softer, huskily tender. He came to her, and took her in his arms. 'It isn't easy to watch you like this.' He kissed her fluttering eyelids with warm lips, rocking her like a child. There was such comfort in his body. 'I hate it, and that makes me sound clinical, as though I didn't care. I do. I care a great deal.'

'Then give me s-something.' She whimpered, digging her fingernails into the hard tendons of his wrist. 'Give me another Methadone, half a Methadone, *anything*!'

'From tomorrow you can have painkillers,' he promised, his mouth in her hair. 'Not until then.'

'*Please.*' She looked up into his face. For the first time since she'd first looked into those intense eyes, there was pity in them. With the intuition of a desperate woman, she clasped her hands round his strong neck. 'For God's sake,' she whispered urgently, her face taut with fatigue. 'Look at me, Adam. Can't you see how b-badly I need it?'

He shook his head wryly. 'The answer's still no.'

'It isn't.' She clung to him, pressing her lips imploringly to the tanned column of his throat. He smelled so good, so warm, so male. 'It isn't, it isn't. I know you want to give me something. You can't bear to see me like this.'

'Oh, pearl,' he murmured, caressing her hair roughly, 'stick it out. You've done so well so far.'

'Please.' The need was overwhelming, she couldn't fight it any more. She had to make him give in to her, any way she could. Yet she had nothing to give, nothing except herself. 'Please, my love, please.' She kissed his mouth feverishly, remembering his desire for her this afternoon. 'You can take anything you want from me. You want me, don't you? You wanted me today, in Darkrising Wood, didn't you?'

'Yes,' he said huskily, 'I wanted you.'

'You kissed me. You said I was beautiful—you must care for me. You wouldn't be doing this if—if you didn't.' Somewhere, from a long way away, she was watching herself coldly, hating herself for what she was doing. Yet she couldn't stop herself. Her face was flushed, taking on a febrile loveliness as she looked up at him with parted, trembling lips. 'I'm no virgin, Adam. You must have found *that* out in all your researches.'

'Don't do this,' he commanded, his fingers biting painfully into her arms. 'It's not you.'

'You don't know me,' she said fiercely. 'How can you say what is and isn't me?' She knew, with a woman's sure instinct, that she was disturbing him, that for all his confident male composure, he was moved by her in some directly sexual way. 'You *do* want me,' she whispered, almost exultantly.

She reached for him, kissing his compressed lips with burning intensity, her own mouth clinging to his. 'Kiss me,' she commanded, certain that he was about to give way. 'Kiss me the way you did in the woods this afternoon.' It didn't matter that she was demeaning herself, that she was tearing down any respect for her he might have. Nothing mattered but getting him to give her what she wanted. If he wouldn't give her medicine, his lovemaking would do, this potent body she was clinging to.

Margot felt him tense in passionate reaction as her

tongue traced the hot outline of his mouth with clumsy provocation.

'Margot . . .' For a dizzying second he was kissing her in return, kissing her with a force and passion that dazed her, the way he'd done in Darkrising; and then he pulled away, breathing fast.

'Why are you holding back?' she asked, her own breath fast and shallow. His face was superbly handsome, the glitter of his eyes reflecting the depth to which she'd stirred him. It was so good to have some control again, after the past days of helplessness. Under her fingers, his body was tensed with power, like a tiger about to spring. 'Because you were Daddy's friend? You aren't my father, Adam. You could be my lover, if you wanted——'

'For drugs?' he asked, eyes darkening with contempt.

'Oh,' she laughed bitterly, her voice raw, 'you say that with such fine morality. Only for drugs! You haven't the remotest inkling how I feel, have you?'

'Did Riff Conroy manage to get you into his bed that way?' he asked firmly. Under his deep tan, she noticed with a wild sense of victory that he was paler now, his mouth a savage line.

'So you know about Riff.' She sat back on her heels, sensing some strange jealousy in him, wanting to hurt him. 'No. I went of my own accord. What was that phrase you used? "A voluntary renunciation."' Her eyes sparkled wickedly. 'I suppose that shocks you.'

'So you were his lover,' he said with controlled fury. His eyes were Arctic slits.

'Yes!' Cruel satisfaction at having hurt him in some way made her heart pound. 'You think I'm a tramp, don't you? So why hold back?' It was a kind of insanity, but she couldn't stop it. Her fingers were shaking as she pulled the white sweater over her head and dropped it on the floor. Her rigid nipples were thrusting against the black silk of the bra that cupped her breasts, and she saw the flicker of raw flame in Adam's eyes as they dropped momentarily. 'Why don't you touch me?' she demanded huskily. 'You know you want to. You could have me, Adam—for so very little.'

'Put your sweater on.' His voice was a ripsaw through timber, harsh enough to make her flinch.

'What's stopping you?' she challenged bitchily. 'Scruples? You didn't have any scruples when you started this circus!'

'Margot,' he said explosively, 'do as I say!'

'Or are you shy?' Spite flushed her cheeks, made her eyes gleam. 'Does it put you off to think I don't want you? Well, maybe I do.' She reached back to the fastening of her bra. 'Maybe I enjoy making love to tall, dark strangers——'

She barely saw him move, but the impact of his palm across her mouth was sharp enough to send stars exploding across her eyes.

For a second she gaped at him, tousled-haired and wide-eyed.

Then something seemed to snap inside her, releasing her. She dropped her face into her hands, feeling the hot tears spill out. What in God's name was she doing, saying? 'No, I didn't. I didn't go to bed with Riff. He wanted me to, and maybe I would have done if I'd been weaker, but——'

He reached for her at last, and held her close, tenderly, kissing her temples. 'God, you frighten me sometimes.'

'Oh, Adam.' Crying had given her release. The madness was ebbing away, leaving her terribly vulnerable. Ashamed of what she'd said and done, feeling as though she'd been broken on a wheel. 'Oh, Adam, I'm so ashamed. Forgive me, I—I don't know how I could have done that. You'll hate me——'

'I won't,' he said, almost smiling.

She took the handkerchief he passed her, and blotted her eyes. 'You'll hate me, d-despise me!'

'Neither of those.' The power had become gentleness now, the danger fading from his eyes as he comforted her. 'If anything shocked me,' he said gently, 'it wasn't the way you were behaving. It was the way I felt.'

He passed her the angora sweater, helped her pull it clumsily on. Almost childlike now, she looked up at him, her cheeks wet. 'But I'm not a virgin. When I was sixteen, I let a boy make love to me at a party ...'

'You don't have to tell me,' he said quietly, wiping the tears from her cheeks with his thumbs. 'That's not my business.'

'I want to tell you.' Shivering again, she reached for him pleadingly. He took her in his arms, cradling her head against his chin, his body warm and strong and protective. Margot clung to him, the words tumbling out. 'I've n-never told anyone. It was in that crazy period. I just wanted to get back at them, for what they were doing to me. I knew this boy, Jeff. He was older than me, and kind of—wild. Like me. He'd been in youth custody, came from a b-broken home. He had tattoos, drove a big motorbike, that kind of thing.' She drew a sobbing breath. 'Th-that made him a kind of hero to me. I got drunk at that party, and I was dancing with Jeff, and I sort of said to myself, *right, you're the one.*' She closed her eyes. 'Losing my virginity was going to be a sort of gesture. A stupid, wasteful gesture——'

Adam stroked her burning forehead, not saying anything, then released her, and passed her the glass of orange juice. She sipped gratefully. This time the liquid was sweet and cool.

'He took me upstairs to an empty bedroom.' The rim of the glass rattled against her teeth, and he reached silently to steady her hand so she could sip again. Her eyes fluttered closed as she re-lived the memory. 'He was so rough, like—like an animal. I wanted him to stop as soon as he'd started, but he wouldn't.'

'My poor Margot,' he whispered, staring at her with a deep compassion in his eyes.

'It was degrading, just awful. And I just lay there, trying to pretend it wasn't happening.' She rubbed her burning cheeks, breathing unsteadily. 'When it was over, he got angry. He said I'd been like a corpse, that I'd made him feel stupid. And then he left.' She laughed shakily, painfully, meeting his serious eyes. 'A nasty little story, isn't it?'

'A sad story.' He seemed to be looking right into her soul with those smoky grey eyes, reaching for some inner contact. 'I take it you didn't tell your mother.'

Margot winced. 'She was too busy getting her divorce from Daddy so she could marry Carl Davison. She didn't have much time to listen to my true confessions, even if I'd been able to tell her.'

'She wasn't that sort of mother?'

'I think she'd given up,' Margot said with tired simplicity. 'We're even further apart now. Since she married Carl, and had Patricia and Jason, she's become almost a stranger to me. There's no self-pity involved, I don't begrudge her her happiness. It's just that she's made herself a new life, and I don't have a place in it.' She looked at him timidly. 'How did you know about Riff?'

'When I spoke to Gill Reynolds, she told me about a small-time drug dealer called Conroy, who was now in jail.' His eyes glinted at her. 'Apparently he'd graduated from pushing heroin outside East End schools to running a profitable manor in central London. Gill said you'd become his lover.'

'That isn't true, I swear it,' Margot said quietly. 'I spent a lot of time with him, but that was because of the research I was doing. Riff was my lead-in to the story I was doing.' She pressed her fingers to her temples, trying to push back the frontiers of the pain. 'Banal, isn't it? I thought I was being so bloody clever. Did Gill tell you why I left *City News*?'

'I had to read between the lines.' He leaned back, surveying her. 'You wanted to do an in-depth story about the London drugs scene,' he guessed. 'They said it was too dangerous, and they couldn't take the responsibility of having you move in those kind of circles.'

'That's not far off,' Margot nodded. 'But I went ahead with the story anyhow. The star cub journalist refusing to be muzzled, and all that.' She smiled humourlessly at her own folly. 'My editor came down like a ton of bricks. So *City News* and I parted company. I—I thought I'd become a freelance.'

'At nineteen?' he said drily.

'Crazy,' she agreed with a tired smile. 'But I thought the story was too important not to write.'

'And Conroy?'

'I'd known Riff vaguely for a couple of years. One of my less savoury acquaintances,' she winced, 'but I knew if I could get him to talk, he'd practically write the story for me. So I started hanging around where he was, trying to get close to him.'

'Just how deep did you get?' he asked, and she was conscious of that deep stillness in him, that almost intimidatingly watchful quality.

'I had more insight than most people into what made kids turn into addicts, Adam.' It hurt to laugh. 'The psychological profile of drug addicts says they tend to be young, rebellious. They also tend to come from broken marriages. Before they start on drugs they usually have a record of petty delinquency, educational failure, emotional disturbance.' Her smile was haunted as she met his darkened eyes. 'Sound like anyone you know? It didn't take me long to get enough material for a story, not with my background. But I never got it written. I didn't bargain on Riff. Once he knew I was writing an article, he didn't want it published. It would have made trouble for him.'

'What happened?' he asked quietly.

With an effort, she controlled her breathing. 'I was at home one morning, writing up the final draft, when the police came round. At first I thought it was about drugs.'

Think you should sit down, Miss Prescott. Major Prescott was involved in an aeroplane crash last night. Middle East. No survivors. Death probably instantaneous. Body to be flown home for burial. Anything we can do . . .

'I was in a kind of trance, I think. I went up to Purley to tell my mother. She'd already heard, and I don't think she really cared. Not after all that time. Neither of them came to the funeral, anyway. When I got back to London I met Riff. I told him what had happened, and he took me back to his flat.' She shrugged painfully, feeling weaker and lonelier then ever in her life before. 'I hardly knew what was happening, Adam. I was—stunned. He got me drunk on vodka. It didn't take much. Then he gave me the heroin. He said it would take away the hurt. Suddenly I wasn't just an onlooker any more. I was a user.' Exhausted, she had to stop again. 'He made sure I got—got enough to want more when I came down.'

'God!' There was cold fury in Adam's face now, the muscles of his jaw knotted. 'The bastard!'

'He's being punished,' she told him tiredly. 'He was arrested a few days after that, in Manchester, and he's been given a seven-year sentence. But I was as stupid as he was wicked; I didn't have to take the stuff, did I? And I managed to rationalise it. I told myself it was all part of my research, that I couldn't really write a Pulitzer-Prize-winning article without personal experience of the stuff.'

'You little idiot,' he said sharply. 'You should have gone for help immediately!'

'I didn't want help.' She looked down at her fingers, twisting them together. 'I still don't want help. I can make it on my own.'

But she could hear the lack of conviction in her own voice, and when he snorted in disgust, she bit her lip in silence.

Adam watched her as she picked up the hairbrush that was lying on the floor, and brushed her tumbled hair with slow, unconscious movements. What was he feeling towards her? she wondered. Despising her? Pitying her?

'I wish I knew what you were thinking,' she said in a small voice.

His smile seemed to warm everything in the room. 'Right now? I was simply thinking how lovely you are.'

She stopped, laying down the brush, and stared at him. It was he, not she, who was beautiful, the most beautiful man she'd ever known. She couldn't analyse her feelings any more, she was too weary. But for the first time that night she was feeling like herself. Not as she had while she'd been on heroin. Like the woman she'd been before the whole nightmare began.

It wouldn't last, she knew that.

'How many women have you had?' she asked naïvely. Adam laughed softly at the question, and she shook her head. 'I know that was a crazy question. But so many women must have loved you, adored you. Did you love any of them?'

'That depends,' he said in a velvety voice, 'on what you define as love.'

'Have you got a woman now? A jealous wife, even?' She tried to find the truth in those dazzling, mocking eyes. 'Does she know you're locked in a cottage, miles from anywhere, with me?'

'If I did have a jealous wife,' he smiled, 'and if she could have seen you ten minutes ago, neither of our lives would be worth a cent.'

She couldn't help laughing. She closed her eyes, listening to the spit and crackle of the fire, remembering the way he'd responded to her just now. Was she glad or sorry that he hadn't ravished her on the carpet, the way she'd deserved?

Something was growing between them, some bond that was deeply, wildly exciting. It stirred nerves deep in her stomach, teased her sexuality, warmed her.

Or was she the only one feeling like that? A man like Adam, able to snap his fingers at any woman he chose, could hardly be expected to get excited over a nineteen-year-old girl. Especially a bird with a broken wing, like Margot Prescott.

But she didn't want to be deflated just yet. She didn't want the bring-down of knowing how stupid she was being. She sighed, just glad not to be in pain.

'You've got quite a way with you,' she said dreamily. 'You draw all my secrets out of me. Like being in a confessional . . .'

'I'm no priest,' he said with an ironic glint.

Margot dropped her eyes. 'I know that,' she said softly.

Adam smiled, lines creasing around his eyes. 'Coming off heroin isn't enough, Margot. It's vital that you realise what went wrong with your life in the past.'

'I'm a handful, aren't I?' There was almost mischief in the glance she gave him from under her lashes. 'Mrs Bell was right, I suspect. I don't think you quite knew what you were taking on.'

The glitter in his eyes was like the flash of a sabre in the sun. 'Perhaps not. Although I knew your father well enough to expect you to have spirit.'

She had a sudden flash of memory. That last time they'd met, in a gloomy London club, he'd told her how impressed he'd been with her work for *City News*. She'd reacted with the bittersweet humour that had always been the hallmark of their relationship. *Hardly your sort of scene, Dad. Taking potshots at the Establishment, I mean.* He'd toasted her across the white linen with a grin. *You're not as unlike me as you imagine, Margot.*

She shook the memory away.

Sleek muscles moved as he uncurled himself and rose to look down at her. 'You're exhausted, sex-bomb. It's time you got some sleep.'

As Margot lay in her bed, later, staring into the darkness, Adam's face haunted her. Though she'd been spilling her heart out to him, she still knew so little about him. About him, or his relationship with her father, or this place, or anything——

She had simply accepted his all-powerful presence as something to hate, something to rebel against. The way she'd been hating and rebelling all her life.

She'd never talked about those things before. Never had to sum them up, see them in perspective. Adam had an uncanny knack of drawing the secrets out of her heart, making her see herself as she really was. Maybe half her trouble, all her life, had been that she'd never thought her problems out enough. Avoided feeling them.

Tears welled up, salty and hot, crawling across her cheeks. Grief was different from self-pity. Self-pity made you a selfish bitch. It was a drug, like heroin, it stopped you from having the slightest interest in anything beyond yourself. You saw the world through a kind of narrow slit, and nothing mattered except your own tiny emotions . . .

A sudden spasm arched through her. She closed her eyes, feeling the gooseflesh spreading across her body, the sickness welling up inside.

'Oh, God . . .'

The remission was over. It was starting again. She hugged her pillow, the way she'd done as a child, gritting her teeth against the trembling that was starting all over again. That shaking pain flared up again, and she fought it down desperately. She mustn't think of it, mustn't acknowledge the way it was racking her.

Think of what he'd said. That the drug would have left her system completely in a very few days. That she'd be whole again, without fear of need. That she'd be free again.

She brought Adam's face into her mind again, trying to

focus on the icy fire of his eyes, the erotic shadows of that so-expert mouth.

What would he look like, naked? Tanned, muscled, utterly, arrogantly male. She curled into a tight ball, imagining him here beside her. Seeing herself worshipping his body, exploring it with possessive hands, tasting his skin, drawing him to her until his love was hers, and he was crushing her against the tumbled sheets ...

The images were deliberately shameless, their force knotting her inside. They kept her from thinking about herself. They burned like a furnace in her loneliness and cold.

'I don't want to eat!' Tearfully, she pushed the plate away, hating him. 'Can't you see I can't keep anything down?' She was exhausted, her spirit overshadowed by a vast black cloud of depression. A spasm of coughing shook her as she limped to the kitchen window, and stared blearily out at the sleeting rain.

The acute agony of last night had receded. But in its place was an almost suicidal emptiness. A non-person, confined and imprisoned and forgotten. She'd never felt this bleak and abandoned. Was no one missing her in London by now? She'd been in this jail more than a week now. Surely to heaven *someone* must have noticed that she was gone?

In her heart she knew that she wouldn't be missed. After all, since she'd started writing the drugs article, her friends had grown used to her disappearing for days on end ...

Her emotions towards Adam had see-sawed irrationally back towards hostility. It was as though he were the only thing she could take her unhappiness out on.

'God,' she croaked, 'I hate this wretched place. I feel so

trapped here.' She coughed painfully again, rubbing her
gooseflesh-riddled arms. 'I want to get away from here!'

'You're losing weight,' Adam said matter-of-factly. He
was leaning against the kitchen table, long legs hugged by
tight denims and tan-coloured boots, a thick fisherman's
jersey emphasising the strength of his arms and shoulders.
The rough clothes made him look even more masculine, if
anything. He assessed her figure with saturnine eyes. 'And
it's coming off the wrong places. I don't want those curves
to flatten out, Miss Prescott. That would be vandalism.'

'I'm not a sex object,' she snapped, not amused by his
tone.

'You won't be a sex object very much longer,' he agreed,
'not if you insist on starving yourself.' With neat strokes,
he quartered an apple, and offered her a red-skinned
crescent. 'You have to try and eat, or your strength will
go.'

'You promised me painkillers.' She swung on him,
feverishly. 'You're a liar! You said I could have painkillers
from today!'

'Did I?' He was unabashed. 'Well. Eat some apple at
least, and perhaps I'll let you have an aspirin.'

Margot's mood was suddenly savage, any truce
between them now over and dead. It was as though any
intimacy between them had never taken place, and all she
could feel for him this morning was bitterness. Her retort
was unprintable. The atmosphere in the cottage was
unbearable, the roughly-plastered walls hemming her in
like a prison. 'I've had enough,' she ground out, glaring at
him. 'I'm bloody well leaving, right now!'

'Indeed?'

'Yes, indeed!'

Adam was utterly composed. He dug the knife into the

scarred pine table and folded his arms. 'Go on, then.'

She turned on her heel, and stalked to the front door, relishing the fight that was going to follow. She was in the mood for a battle royal. At least she'd have an excuse to lash out at him, try and dent that calm façade of his!

He didn't try and stop her.

She pulled an oilskin down from the rack beside the door, tugged it on, and slammed the door behind her. The oilskin was too big, but it at least cut the rain and wind out; underneath, she was wearing only a light cotton top and denims.

Adam didn't follow her as she crunched across the gravel. Was he really going to let her just walk out? She was almost too tense and miserable to care either way. The car was still parked in front of the cottage, but the keys weren't in it. Clever Adam.

Margot followed the road down into the trees, the road he'd driven her up that first night in the Mercedes.

She hauled the hood of the oilskin over her hair, and trudged on through the dripping trees.

There were limits, limits to what she could take. No one had ever made her suffer the way Adam had. No one had the right to do that to another human being. Not even the great Adam, king of wise answers.

The single dull thought in her mind was escape. Making her way to a road. The first thing was to get away from this place, as far away as possible. She glanced briefly over her shoulder. Adam wasn't following. Maybe, incredibly, he would simply let her go.

She plodded on for a few hundred yards. But she was so tired; there seemed to be no energy left in her body. Every joint ached with fire, every muscle seemed to be fibrillating like a broken spring. Suddenly she seemed to be running into an invisible brick wall.

Her legs slowed, becoming leaden. A few more painful steps. Then she couldn't go any further.

Nausea had her doubled over, but there wasn't a thing in her stomach to come up, so she sank slowly on to her knees in the wet gravel, among the falling red and gold leaves. She was too exhausted even to cry.

So this was why Adam had let her walk out. He'd known she simply didn't have the strength to get more than a few hundred yards. Damn him, she thought bitterly, damn him for his knowledge, his certainty.

Margot looked back up the road with blurred eyes. The cottage was way out of sight. She hadn't the reserves of strength to make it back.

She knelt in the rain, shaking weakly, waiting for him.

CHAPTER FIVE

THE rumble of the car came ten minutes later, the wheels crunching on the gravel. She hardly had the heart to lift her head and gaze up at him with pain-darkened eyes.

'I didn't get far, did I?' she whispered.

'Further than I expected.' He lifted her with easy strength on to the seat in front of him, cradling her slender body in his arms. He was warm and solid and strong. She felt like a naughty child being taken home by some patient uncle.

'You must be feeling terrible,' he said calmly, as he helped her off with her oilskin at the lodge. At least there were no recriminations, no mockery in the deep grey eyes.

Weakly, she let him lead her to her bedroom. He towelled her dark hair dry, then helped her take off her wet clothes. The gooseflesh was all over her body, making her skin almost painfully sensitive.

'Lie on the bed,' Adam commanded. 'I'll rub you down.'

She lay face down on the bed, naked but for the black silk briefs she'd put on that morning.

'You're doing well.' She felt the trickle of oil on her back. 'If you'd only stop wasting energy fighting me, and start fighting your symptoms.'

She pillowed her cheek against her folded arms, and let her mind simply go blank.

The massage was deep, strong and confident, his hands expertly easing the cold and the tension out of her muscles.

She lay limply, feeling the knots unwind all over her body as he worked down her back, her hips, her thighs, right down to her heels, bringing warmth and peace.

The desperation ebbed gradually out of her veins.

Only the hissing of the rain outside broke the stillness as he rubbed the warm oil into her skin, and gently traced the curved lines of her hips, the strong, slender muscles of her legs.

Soon she was utterly, dreamily relaxed, even her discomfort about her near-nudity fading. In a strange way, and despite this man's almost overwhelming masculinity, she no longer felt any juvenile bashfulness about her body with him. In a sense, they were becoming lovers. In a sense.

His hands were expert, and very strong. Sometimes, as he came to a tensed muscle, the border between pleasure and pain was very slight.

'I was wrong.' His voice was velvet as his palms slid across her inner thighs. 'Losing a little weight has just made you more desirable. Do you realise that it's been a week since you had heroin?'

She nodded slightly, not wanting to break the spell.

'That's excellent. You're over the worst, and you don't know it.'

She didn't utter the ironic retort that rose to her lips.

'Will you finish the article?' he asked matter-of-factly. 'Once you're well again?'

Margot laughed dreamily. He really expected her to get through this darkness. He really did. 'Oh, Adam.' She opened her eyes and looked up over her smooth shoulder at him. In the cool grey light, his face seemed almost sculpted, as though the flesh and bone had a timeless quality of male beauty. 'You say that so easily ...'

'Rubbing you with oil isn't helping my concentration,' he said with a smoky smile. 'Here.' He passed her the white satin dressing-gown from behind the door, and she wrapped it round herself, feeling terribly weak, but no longer so desperate. She leaned back against the headboard, the silk clinging to the oiled skin, outlining the soft peaks of her breasts, and just stared at him. Until now, she'd been seeing this experience as a pointless excercise in pain. She hadn't believed for a moment that she would really end up free of her dependence. But could she do it?

The possibility was suddenly alive in her. An illuminated exit door from the dark tunnel she'd been in. A glimmer of light, at least. It hadn't really been real to her, not until this moment.

'Ah ...' Through some telepathy, he'd read exactly what she was thinking. 'You've got the message at last, pearl. You're going to be a free woman in a very short time. You're half-way there already. What would you do if I gave you a packet of heroin right now?'

She could only shake her head, not knowing the answer.

'It just—it just seems so impossible.'

'It's not impossible,' he said sharply. 'Difficult, but not impossible. Not unless there's some serious personal instability which is crippling you psychologically. And I don't think there is. I think you've been through a very painful period in your life, yes. But it's over now, and it's time to get back to living.'

'They say that no one gives up heroin,' she said in a small voice.

He made an impatient gesture. 'Thousands of US soldiers became addicts in Vietnam, Margot. Maybe as much as a quarter of the total number. Yet when they returned, all but a tiny fraction of them kicked the habit. Only one per cent of them remained addicts after they'd got back home.'

'London isn't exactly Saigon,' she said tautly. 'I don't have the excuse that I was fighting a war.'

'No,' Adam said brusquely, 'but the Vietnam experience shows one crucial thing—that heroin addiction can be a transient experience in a human life.' He stared into her eyes. 'You understand what I'm saying? It's something that arises when coincidence brings certain factors together.'

She shook her head, hugging her knees. 'Like what?'

'Like intense personal stress, the kind you've been through. Like feeling that nobody loves you. Like having the stuff pushed on you by the Riff Conroys of this world.' He reached for her, fingers biting painfully into her shoulders through the silk. 'Are you listening, damn it?'

'I'm listening,' she said unsteadily.

'Then understand that's what happened to you. And it's over now. You're past the worst.' His eyes held hers with a fierce compulsion. 'You're going to make it, I swear.'

Her gaze was drawn to the watch on his right wrist. No bauble. A gold Rolex, the dial encircled by a fiery ring of diamonds. On any other man it would have seemed effeminate. On him, it was stunning.

Watches like that—and arrangements like this one—didn't come cheap. Everything about him spelled success, achievement. His man's body had a leopard's grace, radiating the same kind of dangerous strength. An overall impression of power. A quality to respect and fear. What was he doing here, wasting his time with a dead friend's daughter who was, after all, just another addict?

'Tell me about your brother,' she asked. 'You said he'd been an addict. What happened?'

Adam's face stiffened. She knew she was treading on forbidden ground, but she suddenly wanted to widen the gap in the wall between them.

'Please,' she said quietly. 'Tell me what happened to him.'

Adam leaned back slowly. His eyes took on an inward look, and again she had that flash of feeling the he belonged to mountains and deserts, pure and remote places. There was something in him no woman would ever tame. 'Very well,' he agreed softly. 'You have a right to know. Michaèl had cancer.' He folded one leg beneath him, resting his elbow on his other knee, and looked absently at her face, as though seeing through her. 'In the bones. They call it osteosarcoma. He was only twenty-three when he died.'

'I—I'm sorry, Adam.' It sounded so lame, but she had to say something, drop some offering into that painful silence.

'They had to use very strong painkillers because he was going out of his mind. Morphine, then heroin.' His mouth tightened in a dry smile. 'Did it ever occur to you how ugly those names are?'

'When you said he was an addict——' She lifted her hands, then dropped them in her lap. 'I—I didn't know that's what had happened.'

'How could you have known? Don't look so tragic. It was a long time ago now. It doesn't sadden me to talk about Michael, *chérie*. He had a worthwhile life.' He rested his chin on his fist, face brooding. 'At the end, after surgery and a long course of radiotherapy, the pain had gone. But the disease had spread, and he had no more than a few months to live. He didn't want to die an addict to heroin.'

'How did he——?' Margot didn't finish the question.

'We went to Corsica together,' he said dreamily, 'just the two of us, for a holiday. Maybe retreat would be a better word. We stayed in a hunting lodge, up in the mountains.' He glanced round with a distant smile. 'A place not unlike this one, remote and tranquil. There we simply sat it out together, talking and waiting and listening to the mountains. He didn't have much physical strength, of course, but he had a strong will and a clear mind. When we came back to our family, Michael was a free man. He was able to prepare himself, and his affairs, to face death with dignity. Thank God, there wasn't much more pain, not even at the very end. He died three months afterwards, at home.'

Margot's eyelashes were wet. 'Was he—was he your only brother?'

Adam smiled that heart-melting smile again. Even though it creased the skin around his eyes and mouth, it seemed to take ten years off him. 'Oh, no. I have two younger brothers and two younger sisters. But Michael and I were always very close. I taught him to ski, to sail, to swim, to drive, to fly——' He drew a breath. 'We were the best of friends.'

He led her to the kitchen, and poured her a bowl of cornflakes. This time she didn't argue, but sat where he ordered, eating in a kind of daze.

'So,' he went on, watching her over folded arms, 'what about that article? You said you were working on the final draft. Are you going to try and get it published?'

'I don't know. The whole thought of drugs terrifies me now ...'

'What about *City News*? Will your job still be waiting for you?'

'I don't think so,' she admitted in a small voice. 'Anyway, I don't know if I'd want to go back, even if they were prepared to take me.'

'What will you do?' he asked seriously.

'*If* I ever get back to a normal life,' she emphasised, 'I'll make a fresh start. Maybe I'll write a novel, or try and get a job in publishing.' She shrugged with an uneasy laugh. 'I'll find something.'

'You'll have to.' His tone was decisive. 'You can't simply drift, not after a thing like this. It's essential for you to resume a normal life.' He paused. 'If you want me to, I'll see what I can do about finding you a job.'

Margot's expression changed. 'Very kind of you,' she said stiffly. 'But I think I'd prefer to do without patronage, thanks.'

'You can't afford any foolish pride,' he retorted, his eyes glinting.

'I suppose you swing a lot of influence, *Mr* Adam?' She found his arrogance so hard to take sometimes. It infuriated her when he talked about her in that possessive, proprietorial way. 'I'm sure you could twist someone's arm on my behalf. It's just that you've interfered with my life far too much already.' Her voice was acid. 'I'd like to sink or swim on my own from now on.'

His brows were a stormy line for a second, and then his expression eased. 'I'd prefer you to swim. In any case, you're not out of the whirlpool yet, Margot. Don't be too arrogant too soon.'

She stared at the puddle of milk in her empty bowl, the conversation still echoing through her mind. Getting back to a normal life. Working again. Getting the strength to face her old friends, make new ones. Could it possibly be within her reach? A few days ago she'd have laughed bitterly at the idea. Now ...

'Maybe I'll rewrite that article, after all,' she said suddenly, looking up at the devastating face she'd come to know so well. 'I know so much more now. Being an addict is like going underground. It's—it's as though your life changes from colour to black and white. You can't think about normal things any more. All you can think about is where your next fix is coming from. You don't take the stuff to feel good. Not after the first few times. You take the stuff to keep from feeling bad.' She picked up her bowl, meaning to take it over to the sink. 'But you have to keep taking more and more. More and more, just to stop feeling as though you're disintegrating.'

The bowl slid through her fingers, splintered on the floor. Abruptly, she was going to cry. She felt the tears surging up inside her, unstoppable and scalding.

'It's just—so—horrible!'

The sobs were explosive, shaking her helplessly. Grief for what had happened to her over these past three months, grief for all the hurt she'd seen and felt, came flooding out of her with the suddenness of an earthquake, choking her throat and eyes. She was numbly aware of Adam's hands steadying her, guiding her back to the chair, and then she was crying against his shoulder, her voice broken and lost. He was her rock, and she clung to him, crying her heart out.

The paroxysm died down after a while, leaving her shaky and weak as a kitten. Adam was stroking her hair, holding her tight.

'I'm—I'm sorry about the bowl,' she said, half-way between a sob and a laugh. 'I'm sorry about everything, Adam. I'm such a fool, I just don't know what comes over me . . .'

'Smash everything in the house, if it makes you cry,' he said gently. 'Tears are your best medicine right now.' Warm male lips touched each of her eyes, blotting the soaked lashes. 'I'll make some tea.' He busied himself with the kettle while she dried her face. She watched him with glistening eyes, feeling closer to him than she'd ever felt to any human being. Her rock, her magnificent, majestic man, making her a cup of tea in jeans and a fisherman's sweater. A pang of desire struck her heart like an arrow; not physical desire, just desire to have this always, this closeness. Whether there were tears or joy, to have him with her to share it.

There had been nothing in her life like this before, no experience so precious as this time with Adam. He was maddening sometimes, one of the most arrogant and strong-willed people she'd ever known; yet even hating him was more vivid and intense than any emotion she'd known. Adam was so strong, so natural. She remembered the way he'd simply kidnapped her off the street, immaculate in that beautiful Burberry coat . . .

Oh Adam, she thought sadly, I've given you so many reasons to despise me. Will you ever learn to see me as a woman—and not just as a bird with a broken wing?

She had a foreboding somehow, she couldn't explain

why, that Adam was soon going to be gone from her life.
The thought filled her with sick pain ...

The next morning dawned beautiful and cloudless, and
Adam drove her up to the Hall.

She'd awoken with little pain, and without that
bursting feeling of tension, and over breakfast she felt
Adam's eyes taking in the touches of colour that had
appeared in her cheeks.

The invitation to come and see the stud farm was tossed
out almost casually, as though he didn't want to rush her
into any decisions, but Margot was surprised at the
eagerness of her own response.

It was the first time she'd been away from the security of
the cottage and Darkrising Wood since she had first
entered them, and it was a strange, almost disquieting
feeling. The worst of her withdrawal pains seemed to have
gone, now. As she sat in the Mercedes beside him, thinking
of that first day he'd picked her up in London, she was
conscious that her body and mind were slowly returning
to a kind of normality.

'Have you ever been to a stud farm before?' Adam
asked as they drove through the woods. Margot shook her
head.

Her first view of the stud was unforgettable.

It was a massive complex of white-walled, grey-tiled
buildings, its back sheltered by Darkrising Wood, its front
looking out across a vista of beautiful green gallops that
stretched into an idyllic landscape.

The buildings formed four large courtyards, covering
at least two or three acres. As Adam guided the car up a
gravelled drive that led through a colonnade of great

trees, a string of gleaming horses, each led by a stable lad, was emerging from the arched main gateway. Wrought iron letters curved overhead, reading: 'Harcourt Hall— The Korda Stud'.

Margot was too flabbergasted to say much except, 'Wow!' She'd imagined something grand, but not this jewel-like beauty. Adam Korda wasn't just rich. He was immensely rich. 'Do you *own* all this?' she asked in wonder.

'More or less,' he said with the ghost of a smile. 'I bought it ten years ago, when it was badly run down, and I've been restoring it ever since.'

The gravel crunched underfoot as they walked across the main yard towards the block signposted 'Reception'. 'Last year I managed to acquire the adjoining land,' Adam went on. 'Several hundred acres in all, no use for agricultural purposes, but ideal for exercising the horses.' He glanced up at the sky 'And for stretching the spirit a little.'

'This is unbelievable,' she murmured to him as they walked through the humming office. 'How has your empire managed without you for the past couple of weeks?'

'It's hardly an empire,' he smiled. 'Bloodstock is an oddly intimate little world. And don't be put off by the computers. They're just a convenient way of storing information about the stud. They save a hell of a lot of paperwork, and it gives a special perspective on the whole business of breeding horses.'

He introduced her to a pretty brunette called Sara Gould, who was in charge of the office. Margot watched the staff of mainly young women as Adam dealt briefly with a list of queries Sara had for him. She was quietly envying their neat, fulfilled lives. She could see the distinct attraction of being one of these pretty young things right now, with no care in the world but a crush on the boss to worry about . . .

The stud exuded busy order. And for all he was casually dressed in faded cavalry twill slacks and shirt, boots, and a clearly well-used hacking jacket, Adam stood out clearly as master in his own domain; Margot couldn't help noticing the respectful way in which the staff, from stable lads to managers, deferred to him, nor the relaxed friendliness with which he responded.

Beyond the computer-equipped offices, more wonders unfolded. Set in an ocean of lawn, formed by a huge L in the stable blocks, stood the main house. It was so perfectly proportioned as to seem almost small in comparison to the long stable blocks, a three-storey Queen Anne country house in quarried stone, the arched windows looking out across the park in neat rows. Beside it was a vast Victorian greenhouse, its glass domes glittering, and beyond that, the dark green mass of Darkrising.

Bathed in the golden sunlight, it was a breathtakingly beautiful sight. Six or seven horses were being exercised in a field to the west of the main buildings, dominated by the great square shadow of the house.

'Is that where you live?' Margot wondered in awe.

'Some of the time,' Adam nodded. 'Though the cottage suits me just as well.' He smiled at her. 'It's also a lot more private.'

She recalled the glances of barely veiled curiosity some of the secretaries had given her. Did the whole stud know that Adam Korda was keeping a raving madwomam locked up in his lodge?

'Do they—know about me?' she asked hesitantly. 'Your employees, I mean?'

'They think you're my cousin,' he said gently. 'Recuperating after a serious illness. No one knows who you really are, or why you're here.'

'That's a small mercy,' Margot muttered. 'What would they say if they knew you'd kidnapped me?'

'What would they say if they knew you'd been a heroin addict?' he countered easily. Bright eyes sparked a challenge at her, and she looked away. 'Come on,' he commanded with a grin, 'and I'll show you some of our best stallions before we see the house.'

They were beautiful creatures, each majestic male kept in gleaming condition, and housed in centrally heated, roomy accommodation that probably rated five stars in the equine world. Not all of them were approachable, but Adam gave her sugar lumps to offer the gentler animals, and it was a strange thrill to feel the velvety muzzles snuffling in her palm, to stroke the gleaming coats.

The yards, Adam told her, had been designed to give the horses the benefit of maximum sunlight and air, together with shelter. Built into the main complex was a fully equipped veterinary laboratory, and even a large indoor pool—not for the staff, but for the horses. 'Swimming happens to be excellent excercise for horses,' Adam smiled in answer to her sceptical expression. 'It's a little too cold at this time of year, but in the summer there's nothing they love better than a swim.'

'They live better than most humans do,' she commented.

'They work harder than most humans do,' Adam retorted, 'and they make a damn sight more money.' He slapped the neck of a big, glossy bay stallion who'd been peering inquisitively over his stable door at them. 'This is Sea Cottage. Six of his first-crop yearlings made over two hundred thousand pounds at Tattersalls last year.'

'What's Tattersalls?' she enquired.

'The top auctioneers at Aintree,' he said, wincing at her ignorance. 'And what's more, his foals have shown really exciting talent on the track this season. He's turning out to be an exceptional sire.'

Margot could see the obvious empathy between man and beast, two splendid male animals sharing a kind of extra-sensory understanding.

'He seems to know you're pleased with him, anyway,' she commented, reaching out to stroke the jet-black mane. 'What made you go into breeding racehorses, of all things?'

He glanced at her in surprise for a moment, then nodded slightly, as though remembering she knew next to nothing about him.

'My family have always been bloodstock breeders, back to the fourteenth century and beyond,' he said gently. 'They were originally of gypsy stock, or so the legend goes, but they settled in central Europe during the Middle Ages. Korda horses have marched in the armies of Popes, raced for the stables of princes across Europe. Even Elizabeth the First owned a Korda stallion.'

He led her through an arched gateway into the next yard, where a group of lads were coaxing a handsome young mare out of a loose-box.

'In the nineteenth century,' he went on, 'the business became very run down. The advent of the motor-car did the rest. Around the turn of the century, my great-grandfather moved to England, and kept the family name and business going, though in a very small way, breeding placid horses for little girls to ride in gymkhanas.'

'You appear to have restored the business to its former glory,' Margot commented softly, glancing at his face.

'I've tried,' he nodded, fierce pride arching his nostrils momentarily. 'Since my childhood, Margot, I had only one real ambition in my mind—to make the Korda stud live again. My brothers are men of the twentieth century.' He shrugged expressively. 'Michael, who died, was a computer wizard. Simon is training to be a lawyer. My sisters are too concerned with husbands and babies. Our father and mother died when we were children.' He met her eyes with that heart-melting smile. 'That left only me—the throwback.'

'Yet you're too complex to be simply a throwback,' she answered his smile. 'You obviously revel in expensive cars, computers, modern things like that. Isn't that a contradiction?'

'Maybe.' He surveyed her mouth with hooded eyes, as though wondering how well she really understood him. 'But I feel there's some inborn impulse in me to work with horses, something inherited from all those generations of my ancestors.'

'Something in the blood?' she asked, only half teasing.

'Why not?' He pointed to a figure in a trilby and sheepskin coat, walking across the yard towards the young mare. 'That man is Billy Shaughnessy, my manager and trainer-in-chief. The Irish are the most experienced breeders in Europe, and I trust Billy's judgement implicitly. His father trained horses, and his grandather before him. It's in his blood, too. I want to show you Macallen, our top stallion. You're not too tired to go on?'

There was concern in his eyes as he took her arm. He tilted her chin up so that he could look into her face. 'Damn,' he muttered, almost to himself. 'I should have known you're not strong enough yet.'

'I'm fine,' she said with a smile, although the unaccustomed exercise had begun to tell on her. His touch meant so much to her. 'I want to see Macallen, Adam, really I do.'

For all his imposing size, the black stallion was as light on his feet as a cat. The stable lad who led him out of the stone archway had pride written all over his snub-nosed features.

He trotted Macallen across the yard, and Margot could only marvel at the fluid, dancing movement of the stallion. Under the gleaming coat, the rangy muscles were perfectly defined, the strength of his long legs belying their slenderness.

Adam's eyes had softened. 'This is Macallen, Margot. Our pride and joy. This year he became Europe's leading sire of two-year-olds, with twenty-seven stakes winners in his first two crops. Has he been for his run yet, David?'

'Not yet, Mr Korda,' came the broad Yorkshire reply, 'He had a gallop across top field last Thursday, but vet's been keeping him in since then.'

'So that's why he's looking a bit indignant, is it?' She watched as Adam ran sure fingers down the horse's leg, murmuring endearments in a soft voice. 'That swelling's right down this morning. I think I'll take him out myself, just for ten minutes. Saddle him up, please, David.' He smiled at Margot while the lad saddled the horse up. 'What do you think of him?'

'He's absolutely beautiful,' Margot said honestly,

watching the proud plumes of steam at the flaring nostrils.
'He must be worth a fortune.'

'What a mercenary idea,' Adam growled. But he looked
amused none the less. 'He's worth a lot, yes. But that isn't
why we love him.' Smoothly, he hoisted himself into the
saddle, tucking his boots into the stirrups. Nervous at first,
the stallion pranced backwards, snorting, but Adam's
hands were like velvet on the reins. He wheeled the big
horse round, and with a click of his tongue set him
cantering across the yard towards the field. The clattering
steel-shod hooves struck sparks off the stone as they crossed
the path. The lad, David, moved to Margot's side as she
walked to the fence to watch.

'He won't let many people ride him,' he said with a
scowl which sat oddly on his adolescent face. 'Since he's
been at stud, he's got out of the way of being ridden by all
and sundry. But Mr Korda can get him to do anything.'

'Is Adam good with horses?' Margot asked.

'What does it look like?' the lad retorted in scorn at her
ignorance.

She watched in silence while Adam broke into a gallop.
He was like a centaur, his hips fused with the beast
beneath him, yet utterly in control of all that pulsing
power. The drumming of Macallen's hooves was like a
pagan tattoo on the earth. There was no hint of roughness
or cruelty, and yet the horse obeyed every movement of
thigh and hand.

The morning light glanced off the stalion's glossy coat,
outlining Adam's lithe body as he crouched over the
horse's back. A wry smile crept across her full mouth.
Korda horses have marched in the armies of Popes, raced for the
stables of princes across Europe. It was easy to see him as a

medieval prince, lance in hand as he urged the black
stallion across the dewy grass with the speed of a striking
hawk.

'Is he kind?' she asked, for no reason she could think of.
'To the horses, I mean.'

'Aye.' David seemed unsurprised at the question. 'You
get a lot of rough people in this business. Horses don't like
it, miss. I've worked with 'em all me life, and I know.' The
boy, who must have been all of sixteen, was following
Adam with intent eyes. 'He never gets impatient nor
forces them to do anything they don't want to. They just
obey him. Uncanny, like. He can get them to do
anything.'

'I see,' Margot said gravely. 'Is he a good boss?'

'He's all right.' The boy's mouth closed like a trap, and
she had to hide a smile. Behind that fierce scowl, she
realised, David the stable lad was hiding a bad case of
hero-worship. 'What d'you think of the horse, miss?'

'The horse is beautiful,' she nodded. And so is the man,
she added silently to herself. More beautiful than any
horse could ever be, more alive, more wonderful. 'Are all
the horses here Adam's?'

'Most of 'em. Mr Korda puts his own mares to the stud
stallions, miss.' He looked at her to see if she'd understood.
'That cuts down on the number of visiting mares, but it
shows what kind of man he is. He's got confidence in his
stock, you see. He's not in this game just for the money.'

'It doesn't look as though he needs any more,' she
commented, looking at the immaculately kept
surroundings.

'He doesn't. He's the best.' David nodded his tousled
head at Macallen. 'That horse made over a million in

prize money, miss. And that's peanuts compared to what he's making at stud.'

It wasn't difficult to put on an impressed expression for the lad. When Adam finally galloped the horse up to her, his dark hair had been swept back from his forehead, and his eyes were glittering with enjoyment. 'He runs like the wind,' he grinned, reining in in front of them. The steam was clouding at his mouth as he panted slightly. 'No sign of that strain. I'll get the vet down to check him this afternoon. Do you ride, Margot?'

'I don't ride horses like that,' she laughed nervously, overwhelmed by his sheer male presence.

'You will do,' he promised.

The thought hit her with sudden force. *I've met my man.* It wasn't a feeling of subjugation, of being dominated. It was something much deeper, something that touched her heart. In Adam, she had found a man who could make her do anything. A master, perhaps, but more than a master. A man who could lift her to the greatest heights she would ever achieve.

Still dazed by that moment of recognition, she reached out a tentative hand to touch Macallen's sleek, powerful shoulders.

'He's good-tempered, don't worry,' said Adam, reaching into his pocket. 'He ought to be, considering the life he leads. Give him this.'

Margot took the sugar lump Adam passed down to her, and held it out in her palm. Macallen's muzzle was moist with steam as he snuffled it up. His eyes were indeed sweet-expressioned, unlike the rather savage look she'd seen in some of the stallions' eyes. 'He really is beautiful,' she repeated in awe. There was always something dominant about a man on a horse; when it was a man like Adam, it took your breath away. Her man. She would always belong to him, she felt that as surely as she knew she was standing here before him. But would he ever—*could* he ever—belong to her?

'We'll find one of the gentler mares for you to learn on. But maybe not today.' Adam passed the reins to David, and slid down fluidly. He gave the horse's neck an affectionate slap. 'Take him back to the stables, please, David.'

'Did you enjoy that?' she asked as the lad trotted away with the stallion.

'I did.' Hands on hips, Adam arched his back with a grunt. 'I haven't been on a horse for weeks.'

'Too busy with me,' she suggested. He'd looked so magnificent on horseback that it was almost an effort to banter with him now.

'Maybe.' He straightened, meeting her eyes with a directness that made her heart contract. 'We'd better get back to the cottage. You've got an appointment with the doctor at two-thirty.'

CHAPTER SIX

THE doctor was blonde, very attractive, and in her mid-thirties. Her name was Christine Gollings, and she told Margot during the course of a very thorough examination that although hers was basically a rural practice, she'd had detailed experience of drug addiction in Liverpool, in her first surgery.

And although it was Margot's first real chance to complain to a responsible third party that she was being held prisoner here against her will, she didn't do so. She wouldn't have dreamed of it.

Dr Gollings, indeed, seemed to assume that she'd come here of her own free will.

'In many ways,' she murmured, listening to Margot's chest, 'you've chosen the hardest way of doing it. But also the best. You've been a very brave woman indeed.' She slipped the stethoscope off and made a note. 'Your chest's still a bit rattly. That's to be expected. It's not really worth giving you anything, as long as you keep coughing it all up.' The handsome blue eyes were unexpectedly penetrating. 'You're not going to be tempted back to heroin, are you? There's a very serious risk of pulmonary oedema, you know. I've seen addicts who died so quickly the needles were still stuck in their veins.'

'You don't have to terrify me,' Margot said gently, pulling her shirt down. 'I'm not going back to heroin.' The words were out before she'd thought about them.

'You sound as though you mean it.' The blonde doctor looked really pleased. Oh, I do, Margot thought tiredly. Now that I have something to live for, I do.

'I should really send these notes to your GP,' said Dr Gollings, glancing at Margot. 'But I won't if you don't want me to.'

'I'd rather keep it private,' she said, thinking of old Dr Simpson. 'My GP probably isn't as comfortable with drug addiction as you are.'

'I see. We can talk about it later, in any case.' The doctor put the notes away. 'And you?' she said quietly. 'Are you comfortable with yourself?'

'I'm not sure what you mean,' Margot said.

'I mean that your self-image seems to be low. Do you feel that because of your addiction you've lost a part of your self-respect—even your self-trust?'

Margot looked at her own hands, the nails plain and unvarnished. That was the way she felt right now. Plain and unvarnished. Like a silk blouse that had somehow found its way through the wringer. She glanced up at the doctor with a slight shrug. 'I don't exactly feel proud of myself, no. I've been almost incredibly stupid, and it's rather a jolt to discover just how idiotic you can be.'

'Do you trust yourself?' the doctor pressed. 'Trust yourself to carry on with a normal life, I mean?'

'I think so.' How could you explain the shame and regret to a stranger? Not that Christine Gollings' presence embarrassed her. There was only one person with whom she felt ashamed of herself. The man who'd seen her through every humiliation and shadow of detoxification. The man who knew her better than anyone had ever known her. Could he ever respect her again? It wasn't her own trust she doubted. It was Adam's trust in her.

'I expect Adam has been a great help?' the doctor said, as though picking up her thoughts.

Margot drew a breath. 'He's been——' She couldn't find a word.

'Quite.' By the expression on Dr Gollings' bee-stung mouth, she obviously suspected that Adam was Margot's lover, but was too diplomatic to ask.

'Adam and my father were good friends,' Margot said with a slight smile. 'That's the only reason he's interested in me. I met him for the first time when he—er—invited me up here. I know hardly anything about him.'

'Yes, he explained about your father. I'm sorry about that. His death must have been a bad shock for you.' Dr Gollings looked as though she didn't quite know how to phrase what she was going to say next. 'The thing is that, with going straight on to heroin, you haven't had time to grieve properly yet. If you know what I mean. That may explain why you're prone to depression now—delayed grief over your father's death, which only happened a few months ago, after all. I'm not a psychologist, but I'd advise you not to hold back any feelings of grief. Just let it out.' She gave Margot a bottle of paracetamol tablets, and started packing her bag. 'Adam tells me you cry rather easily. That's probably a good thing, don't you think so?'

'It brings relief,' Margot nodded.

'Adam's a remarkable man,' the doctor said, 'as I expect you've already gathered. He has a fantastic capacity to inspire people, which I suppose explains all the millions. How did he persuade you to try and come off heroin?'

'He didn't give me much choice,' Margot said absently, thinking about what the other woman had said. 'He must be a millionaire many times over.'

'Anyone who's interested in horses between Kentucky and Hong Kong knows about Adam Korda,' the doctor smiled. 'His family have been great bloodstock breeders for God knows how many centuries.' She patted Margot's arm. 'If you're going to be staying here much longer, I hope you like horses. Anyhow, you seem to have come through detoxification extraordinarily well, Margot. You've achieved something beyond the normal. I don't say that lightly, either. You've got something to be very, very proud of. Just keep going the way you are, and you'll never look back.' She snapped the bag shut, and untied her golden hair from the severe pony-tail. Suddenly she looked younger, and much more feminine. 'I'll see you again in a few days. Remember what I've told you—keep warm, and keep eating and drinking. And don't be worried about the dreams. There's a rebound of REM sleep that can last for a couple of months . . .'

Margot followed the doctor out of her bedroom, listening with half a mind to the advice she was being given. Until today, she hadn't ever thought of Adam Korda as having a life beyond this cottage, and her. What she'd found out this morning had been thrilling—yet it had also been frightening . . .

'Well,' Adam enquired, 'how do you think she is?'

'She's been through a great deal,' Christine Gollings told him seriously. 'She's shown exceptional courage. I've checked all her vital functions, and I don't think she's going to have any physical problems—but she still needs a lot of rest, and a lot of time to get back her full strength.'

'I think we can provide that,' said Adam solemnly. 'And the long-term prognosis?'

'That's up to Margot.' With a pang of irony, Margot noted the melting way Christine Gollings was looking at Adam. Did he have this effect on all women? 'You were right about her, Adam. She isn't an ordinary person at all. She strikes me as having a great deal of quiet strength. I think she's going to come through.'

'Oh, she will. I never had any doubt,' Adam purred, with a slow smile that was meant for Margot alone. 'I never had any doubt at all.'

But Margot was brooding silently, curled in her chair. Oh yes, she was almost cured now. And her problems had only just begun.

When Adam had first brought her to this place, she had hated him. Now she didn't know what she felt for him. But above all her confusion, one thing was certain. She didn't want to accept that this precious time would ever have an end.

She wanted to stay here with him, hating him, loving him, quarrelling with him, being close to him, for ever. She didn't want to find out anything that might take him away from her. Didn't want to discover the thousand things in his life that would come between her and him— women, work, amusements abroad. Like when you were a child, shutting your eyes and hoping the fear would go away . . .

His life was so rich, so complete. And hers? She'd scarcely begun her life, and had damn near botched that beginning, too. She had so little. No job, no family to speak of, nothing. Did she really have anything to offer him?

The days that followed were filled with a growing sense of wonder for Margot.

London was like another world to her now, half forgotten. Her addiction had faded into nothing, leaving her free to think about herself for the first time.

And Christine Gollings had been right—she had needed to grieve for her father, and that brought a great relief of emotions inside her. After so much unhappiness, life was beginning to hold joy for her again. It wasn't simply that she was coming out of the shadows of addiction, and that her dependence on heroin was fading into memory; that feeling she'd had up at the Hall was growing into something deep and potent inside her.

It had unlocked something in her heart, and with the first sprinkling of snow, and the last of the golden leaves, words came to her.

And she'd never talked so much in her life before; a great pouring-out of words that he never seemed to tire of listening to. Experiences, secrets, memories of her childhood. Wandering through Darkrising, or learning to ride on one of the mares up at the stud, she would find herself telling Adam things she thought she'd forgotten, things she'd never believed she could tell anyone.

The exercise helped her to regain her strength even more quickly. When Christine Gollings came to look at her for a second time, she told Margot that she was almost ready to resume a normal life. She commented, too, on Margot's improved mood, and the self-confidence which was beginnning to show in her eyes.

But her deep-seated fear that Adam would always regard her with contempt, or at best with pity, was still there, just beneath the surface of her security.

Late one afternoon after that, Adam lifted the fly-fishing rod down from its place on the pantry wall, and took her down to the river. The sunset was like an immense stained-glass window over the river, the evening soft and mild.

It was extraordinary to be standing thigh-deep in the middle reaches of the fast-moving and probably icy water, and yet not to feel the cold. The rubber waders he'd given her were cosy and warm, for all they were a size too big, and the same applied to the Barbour coat that smelled vaguely of his body.

As she stumbled on the crunchy pebbles underfoot, he steadied her.

'You'll scare the fish to death,' he growled. 'The whole point is to be silent and cunning.'

'Sorry,' she whispered. She took the rod he passed her, sensing the light whippiness of the hand-built cane. The river swirled around their thighs before surging over the outcrop of rocks a little downstream. Beyond, it broadened into a sweep of silver water like a miniature lagoon.

'They're still rising to the fly at this time of year,' he told her conspiratorially. 'Anything that lands on the surface of the water stands a chance of being snapped up by a hungry salmon. Ever done any fishing before?'

'I once caught a perch on the Thames,' she said lamely. 'Daddy baited the hook.'

The barest tilt of an eyebrow expressed total scorn. 'Fly fishing is different. We don't mess around with slimy things like maggots. In fact, we don't use any edible bait at all.' He showed her the fly. It was an exquisite thing, a confection of tiny speckled feathers made to look like a small insect. The hook, sharp as a needle, curved back under the 'tail'.

'That's a nasty little trick,' Margot couldn't help saying ruefully.

'It is rather, isn't it?' He considered the hook with an expert eye. 'Delicious to look at, deadly to sample. Rather like some women I've known. Right, see if you can get it to land under that tree, across by the other bank.'

She swung the rod as he directed her, and the fly splashed clumsily into the water a few feet away.

Adam grunted derisively. 'Never mind. I'll make a fisherman of you yet.'

'Fisherperson.' She shot him a glance from below lowered lashes. 'And that comment about women was sexist in the extreme.'

'All right, fisherperson. Watch.' He whipped the rod in a long arc, and line looped over their heads, thirty feet through the evening air. The fly settled with barely a ripple on the surface of the water. Instantly, there was a swirl in the water beneath, and the fly bobbed for a few seconds before coming to rest. 'There he is,' Adam muttered. 'The old rogue himself. I've been trying to catch him for three years. But he's suspicious. He doesn't believe you get anything for nothing in this life.'

'He's right.' Margot watched the spot in fascination. Adam let the fly drift for a while longer, then started reeling it in.

It was one of the most beautiful spots she'd ever been in, with a vast, timeless tranquillity. The trees along the bank were shedding their crimson leaves into the water, one by one; half a mile downstream, an old stone bridge spanned the river. After that, there was a bend in the river, and the great woods beyond.

'Do you own all this?' she asked quietly.

'Down to the bridge,' he nodded, concentrating on the rod.

She watched the way his body moved as he cast out again, supple, strong and elegant. 'All this time you're spending on me, Adam,' she said quietly. 'How can you afford it?'

'I spend a couple of months each year just sailing.' He re-tied the fly, eyes narrowed with concentration. 'I've never let my work dominate me, Margot. If you do, success becomes just an illusion. I value my own independence too much to let anything tie me down.'

'Does that apply to women, too?' she couldn't help asking.

His expression was amused. 'Your sense of curiosity seems to be reviving.'

'It was just that little crack about the women you've known,' she said, her cheeks colouring faintly. 'Is that how you see the female sex? Pretty, but intent on trapping men?'

'I didn't say *all* women,' he reminded her. 'Only some women.'

'Yet you must have had so many women,' Margot challenged. 'A man like you—you must have wounded some of them? Maybe all of them?'

'We're here to kill a salmon,' he said, the veiled smile his only reproof for her probing. 'Try again.' His arms were strong around her, guiding her hands on the rod. This time, the fly sailed gracefully overhead, and plopped into the still water a respectable distance away. 'Much better,' he judged. 'Now leave it there, and we'll see if you've fooled the old fellow.'

She watched the fly on the twilight river, waiting for

that hungry swirl under the water. The click-click of the reel was a soothing sound. She'd never known how peaceful fly fishing could be, in the immense calm of this sunset.

She hadn't realised he was studying her until he said softly, 'At last you're beginning to look like you should.'

'What?' she laughed, turning to him. 'In green waders and your cast-off fishing-jacket?'

'No. Clear-eyed and healthy, with colour in your cheeks.'

The expression in his eyes jolted her. Her smile faded. Was he telling her it was coming to the time for her to leave? 'I—I still feel terribly weak,' she said truthfully. 'Don't forget what Christine said about the rest I'm going to need——'

She broke off on a gasp as the rod bucked in her hands. She barely had the presence of mind to grab hold of the cork handle before the reel exploded into a long excited buzz as the line surged out.

'You must have hooked the old rascal himself!' Adam said in awe as the quivering tip curved like a bow. The glinting line was racing from the reel as though an outraged water demon were on the other end.

She pushed the rod at him. 'You take it,' she said, half-way between terror and excitement.

'He's your fish,' Adam grinned. 'Nothing to do with me.'

'But—but—what must I *do*?'

'Better slow the reel down before he runs away with all your line, for one thing.'

'*How*?'

'With your hand.' The friction burned her palm, but the line slowed down in its headlong rush. 'Good,' he nodded. 'Now try and reel him in.'

She could never have believed a fish would possess such strength. For every few inches she managed to reel in, the furious salmon seemed to claim back as many yards. And despite her pleas, Adam refused to take the rod over. He was content to watch her with an amused glitter in his eyes, giving her laconic advice.

'Don't let him get beyond those rocks, or he'll snap your line like cotton. Don't let the line go slack. Keep it tight so he can't jerk.'

Within the first few minutes she was exhausted. The battle was steadily going to the salmon. Margot wasn't used to this kind of exercise, and her back and shoulder muscles were aching. 'I can't hold him,' she panted. 'He's going—to get—away!'

'Don't you dare,' growled Adam fiercely. 'I've been trying to hook this one for years. Keep the rod up, girl!'

She'd die rather than let him down, even over something like this! Almost out of breath, Margot strained at the fishing rod, which was as potent as a live thing in her inexpert hands. Fifteen yards away, the water exploded into a silver arc as the salmon leaped clear. She caught a glimpse of a speckled, bullet-smooth flank, and then the fish was gone, hauling at her line with vicious strength.

'God, he's big!' she gasped.

'You're bigger.' Adam reached out and flicked a catch on her reel. 'Start pulling him in now, Margot. Haul on the rod, then reel in, haul and reel in. Keep doing that as long as you can.'

She obeyed, her heart pounding. It felt as though she were trying to pull a steam locomotive along a track. But the fight had slowly swung her way; the struggling fish was inevitably being drawn closer to them.

'Keep going,' Adam commanded urgently. 'Don't give up now.'

She was almost ready to drop by the time the salmon was within striking distance. Adam waded towards the thrashing water with the net at the ready, while she tried to keep the fish from racing off again. The rod was bent almost double, she could hear the cane creak in her straining fingers.

'Quickly,' she begged, knowing her strength was all but exhausted; her arms felt like tired spaghetti now.

'There.' In one fluid movement, he'd netted the salmon. The mightly pull was gone from the rod.

Once the great fish was in the net, the fight seemed to go out of it. Apart from a few surging movements, it lay still, the gills gasping in the cold air.

'I think you've just about worn each other out,' Adam said gently. There was a strange expression on his face as he held the yard-long salmon tight against his chest, and eased the hook from its gaping jaws.

Feeling as though she'd just run an Olympic mile, Margot waded wearily towards him. The salmon was a magnificent creature, gleaming silver and brown, smooth-muscled as a torpedo, with an iridescent sheen to the fine scales. Its eyes were like jewels, the pink gills still gulping wildly in the choking air.

'How beautiful,' she whispered, pressing close to Adam's arm, staring into the net.

'Your fish,' he said huskily, staring into her eyes. 'It was a good fight.'

'You are going to let him go?' she said, almost pleadingly.

'Yes.' He touched the gleaming flank. '*À bientôt, mon vieux*.'

She watched, feeling a sudden burst of delicious happiness inside as Adam lowered the fish under the water, holding it there. The sun was almost gone, the sky a shimmering swathe of violet in the east, velvet-blue overhead.

The salmon gulped in the cold water for long seconds, only its fins stirring, as though scarcely able to believe its luck. Then, with an eruption of sleek strength, it surged out of Adam's hands, heading like a silver harpoon towards Margot's legs.

With a yelp, she tried to step back. The river-bottom was pebbly, and before she knew what was happening, she collapsed backwards into the icy water. Wetness was an instant, unpleasant shock to the system.

Acutely conscious of her indignity, she floundered wildly, trying to stand up, then sliding waist-deep again.

She felt Adam's fingers close round her wrists, hauling her upright. Spluttering, she wiped her eyes. Her clothes were soaked and heavy around her, even her hair wet and icy around her cheeks.

'You *dare* laugh——'

'Not even a chuckle, word of honour,' he grinned, steadying her. 'You haven't lost my best fly-rod, have you?'

Suddenly helpless with giggles, she groped for the rod. Laughter was bubbling out of her the way tears had come only a few days earlier.

'Here it is.' She passed him the dripping thing. 'I'm awfully sorry ...'

'Don't be sorry. You happen to be rather marvellous at the moment.'

Something in the husky tone of his voice made her look up quickly. His eyes were dark with sudden desire, the laughter ebbing out of them.

'Adam——' she started to say, but whatever the sentence was, she never got it finished. He was pulling her close, oblivious of everything, his mouth seeking hers.

She'd kissed Adam before, but not like this. It was as though they'd both been waiting for this moment for a lifetime, desiring it, aching for it—yet leaving so much unacknowledged, so many words unsaid.

His warm lips moved with expert gentleness against the smooth wetness of her own, teasing her mouth open. The delicious warmth that spread through her body made a mockery of any cold she was feeling. Margot lifted her arms to cling meltingly round his neck, moulding herself against his lean, muscular body.

She suddenly felt so weak that the river might have washed her away, had Adam not been there to stay her with his rock-like strength. Here, in mid-stream, mutual desire had locked them together in impregnable safety.

There were no words, just kisses that deepened as they repeated themselves, gentle mouths that explored one another's faces, tasted each other's burgeoning passion.

He kissed her with an intensity that was like nothing any man had ever given her, devouring her soft lips, the delicate femininity of her tongue, savouring her skin and hair as though she were the most beautiful flower, filled with nectar that he had to have.

Like something that had been denied sunlight, Margot felt her soul expanding its wings in the warmth, her fingers hungry as they ran through his thick hair, trailed down the rough stubble of his cheeks ...

Kissing was an ectasy, kissing was a torment. It showed her what had been hidden in her emotions for so long, yet it also showed her so much more to desire. The caress of his lips was intoxicating at her temples, the yielding sweetness of her mouth, the slender column of her throat. When he whispered her name, she looked up dizzily into his face, knowing that he was feeling the same drugged sensuality right now.

The late-afternoon sunlight had brought out the full golden tan of his skin, his eyes a deep, glowing grey that contrasted heart-stoppingly with the thick black lashes and the sweep of black hair. She knew she would never see a more beautiful man in her life again. And inside, that recognition was there again, stronger and deeper than before. Adam Korda was her man. There would be no other, and if she could not possess him, make him hers for life, then the rest of her days would be barren and empty.

'This is crazy,' he said roughly, turning to grope for the newly lost rod. 'We're both going to catch our deaths out here.'

'Yes,' she said numbly. She had to cling to him to avoid foundering in the current. What in God's name was happening between them? Was this what love meant, this terrible, sweet weakness inside?

She was slowly becoming conscious of how icy her legs were. Her waders were full of bitterly cold river, and she squelched as she moved. She started to shiver. 'God, I'm f-freezing!'

'I'm not surprised.' His voice was still almost harsh, as though he wanted to cancel out what had just happened. But nothing could ever do that. 'November's no time of year to go swimming, pearl. Come on.' He gave her an arm to hang on to as they waded back to the bank together. She was so happy, happier than she could remember being.

'Are you jealous because I caught a fish and you didn't?' she murmured against his hard shoulder.

'Beginner's luck,' he scoffed. He hoisted her up in his arms as they reached the muddy shallows, carrying her slender frame as easily as though she'd been a sleepy child going to bed. His strength never failed to thrill her, and she clung to his shoulders, her head pillowed against his hard chest, lost in bliss. 'What concerns me more is you getting pneumonia,' he said gruffly.

She shivered realistically to dig for additional sympathy. She would gladly have risked pneumonia right then, double pneumonia, if it meant prolonging that dazzling kiss . . .

She was shivering in earnest by the time they got back to the cottage, the cold striking into her.

'A hot bath,' Adam decided firmly. 'Get in the tub, and just soak. I'll light the fire and get something for us to eat.'

She ran her bath, pulled off the soaked clothes, and got in. It was sybaritic bliss to lie in the steaming hot water, feeling the ache in her muscles where she'd strained them in the struggle with the salmon, the ache in her emotions where Adam's passion had touched her. What did he feel? Was it the momentary lust of a virile man? Or did it, as with her, go deep into the very soul?

Perhaps after they'd eaten he would take her in his

arms like that again, kiss her in that same heart-stopping way . . .

She closed her eyes, remembering his mouth, the feel of his body against her. Adam was becoming a part of her. And that wasn't just a figure of speech. He was in her blood, in her heart, in her soul. What she felt for him was an amalgam of desire, awe, adoration, need. He was becoming her obsession.

Her body felt tired, weak. But it felt whole. Of the ordeal she'd gone through these past days, almost nothing remained. Like the salmon, she, too, had been reprieved, had received mercy at Adam's hands. She saw again the silvery flanks, imagined it swimming free in the dark waters out there. Would there be a scar where that sharp little hook had bitten into the clean flesh?

Like the salmon, she'd been tied by a hook to certain death—until Adam had freed her. And like the salmon, she bore almost no evidence of what she'd been through. She, like the salmon, was free. She'd sworn no oaths, made now vows. She didn't have to. She knew she would never return to drugs, not in any form.

She was not the same woman she had been, a mere three weeks ago. She was altered, utterly changed. Three weeks ago she'd been dying. Walking, talking, apparently alive—but dying inside, every day, with every little white packet she bought——

The thought of heroin was horrifying now. There was no craving, no hunger in her. Instead, she felt a revulsion that was almost savage in its intensity. That self-destructive urge was gone.

She soaped her naked body slowly, thinking of the way Riff had urged her to try heroin, again and again. *Go on,*

Margot. You'll love it. It'll blow your mind. How can you write about it if you've never even tried it?

She'd always refused, always been strong enough to say no. After all, the evidence of what it did to people's lives was all around her. She'd always known how evil it really was.

He'd simply waited for his chance, knowing that once she was hooked, the story she was writing would be doomed. The night she heard that her father had died, Riff had turned her into an addict. As simple as that, with as little feeling.

No, she didn't have to take it. She'd just been too dazed to think . . .

What Riff had done to her, and to others like her, was little short of murder. Murder for gain. Why in God's name had she stayed close to such a dangerous man?

For the first time in months she was able to remember clearly how it had all begun. Riff Conroy had been a little like Jeff. Like Jeff, he'd been dangerous in a very real sense. He'd spat in the face of society, flouted the law. Even while she saw and wrote about the dreadful effects of his trade, she'd felt a sneaking schoolgirl fascination for him. The fascination of the rebellious teenager for the anti-social misfit.

Crazy.

Beside Adam, how insignificant he seemed! There wasn't a man in her world who could come close to what Adam did for her. Where Riff, with his mean cunning, had almost destroyed her, it had been Adam Korda who had recreated her. Made her a woman again.

Remembering that kiss, out in midstream, made her

body respond with a flood of renewed desire. God, how she wanted him!

There was more power in Adam, more warmth and goodness and creative energy, than in anyone she'd ever known. She wanted him. She wanted him utterly, to have his body and his mind for her own. To bear his children in her womb, to be his lover all her life.

To be his woman, as he was her man.

She rinsed her smooth skin. Could it happen? It was something she wanted with an urgency that was almost frightening. And she could do it. Maybe.

But how much longer could she postpone their parting? He'd wanted to talk about her getting another job again this morning. He'd talked about her future.

Her future.

She clambered out of the bath, pink and clean, and towelled herself dry. She didn't want to think of a future outside of this woodland, outside of Adam.

She brushed her hair until it gleamed as iridescently dark as a raven's wing, then stared at her own face in the mirror. Was she beautiful? She had been called that once. The bones of her face were good, her eyes and mouth striking, passionate. But could she ever compete for his attention with the beautiful, sexy, clever women who must crowd around him every day of his life? Those beautiful, barbed creatures?

She wanted to show him how well she was, show him she could be trusted. Show him she was worthy of his love . . .

Her handbag was still lying on the little desk in her bedroom, where she'd left it days ago. She padded to her bedroom, wrapped in her towel, and opened it with a thoughtful expression. She hadn't used any kind of cosmetics for weeks. He'd seen her at her worst, with scrambled hair and white face, about as alluring as a scarecrow.

She emptied the bag on to her bed, poking through the miscellaneous contents. A lipstick, mascara, eyeshadow, her little flaçon of *Diorissima*. Not exactly an arsenal, but better than nothing.

Making-up was like performing a forgotten ritual. The touch of colour at her lips and eyes added a sudden tension of beauty to her face. She had nothing to colour her cheeks, but she wasn't interested in deceiving him, in any case. He knew her too well for that. She just wanted to make him notice her.

For the first time, too, she did something different with her hair, tying it loosely back with a scrap of ribbon, letting two wings drop forward to frame her face.

The white angora sweater she'd worn on that first day was washed and clean in her drawer. It had strong, bittersweet memories for her—maybe for Adam, too? She picked up a grey skirt to go with it, wanting her clothes to be simple and elegant, the way she'd like to be.

Suddenly, her heart was beating against her ribs. She went to find Adam.

CHAPTER SEVEN

HE'D lit four slim rose-candles, and their romantic light glowed on the immaculately laid table like an echo from a time when this house was young.

There was even a spray of flowers in the middle, late autumn flowers; already a few petals had fallen on to the scarred pine.

'Wow,' Margot said quietly, closing the door behind her.

'Celebration dinner,' commented Adam from the stove. 'Your first salmon should not go unmarked.' She caught a glint of his smile. 'We'd be eating the old fellow himself, except for your sentimentality.'

'*You* let him go,' Margot pointed out.

'Anyway, we're going to have to put up with steak.' He'd changed into slacks and a black sweater; the clothes hugged the long muscles of his legs, emphasised the hard male lines of his body. 'Don't just stand there dreaming,' he reproved. 'You'll find wine in that rack over by the fireplace.'

She picked a bottle of claret, hoping she was doing the right thing. Adam lifted the steaks out of the marinade and laid them into a hot pan. With the fierce sizzling, a delicious herbal aroma filled the kitchen. She was ravenous all of a sudden, and when, after a few minutes of turning, the steaks were ready, she ploughed in with the appetite of a healthy young animal.

'Fantastic,' she judged, her mouth full. 'This makes up for falling in the water!'

'Perhaps that was old Foxy's idea of revenge,' he smiled, filling her glass with the ruby-red wine.

'Foxy?'

'The salmon. After all, to be hooked by a rank beginner . . .'

'There,' she said, cutting up the succulent meat, 'I knew you were jealous.' He'd made a salad, too, and the fresh things were clean and sweet on her palate. Her enthusiasm for the food didn't go unnoticed.

'I've never seen you eat like this,' he commented, grey eyes warm on her. 'You're not even chewing!'

'And there I was, determined to be so sophisticated tonight,' she said ruefully. 'You cooking's undone all my plans.'

'Sophisticated?' He studied her over his wine glass. 'Is that how you think I want you to be?'

'Well, you're no innocent,' she smiled. 'I don't see you as the sort of man to be fascinated by the freckly schoolgirl type.'

'The type who falls in the river?' he enquired, one eyebrow lifting gently.

Margot flushed, turning back to her steak. 'That sort of thing. I just wanted to be a little less of a walking disaster-area tonight.'

'Ah. That explains the lipstick and the perfume.'

So he *had* noticed, despite the candlelight. Her heart stangely unsteady, Margot concentrated studiously on her food. 'Don't you approve?'

'You look very beautiful, if that's what you want me to say.' Adam traced the shape of his glass with slim, strong fingers. 'But then you'll always be beautiful to me.'

His words seemed to turn her heart over inside her. She didn't have an answer ready, just gulped at the strong wine, feeling its noble bouquet fill her mouth.

'When did you first meet my father?' she asked, turning back to her food.

'For the first time? Six years ago.'

'In the Gulf?' Margot guessed.

'In the desert,' he nodded.

She looked up. 'What were you doing in the Gulf?' she asked curiously.

'Shopping,' he smiled. 'I buy horses all over the world, Margot. I'm always on the lookout for new blood, new sources of stock. I like Arab horses for their temperament and grace, and at that time I was buying in the Gulf states.' He paused for a moment, almost hesitating. 'As it happened, your father saved my life.'

'Daddy?' she echoed in astonishment.

'Yes,' he replied gently. 'Your irresponsible father. I was travelling through a neighbouring state at the time, making for the provincial capital, when our little party strayed into a particularly nasty little tribal war.'

'You're joking!'

'Hardly. We'd thought we were in a safe part of the country, but the country was running out of safe parts by then. We were taken hostage by guerrillas.' He smiled drily at her expression. 'It was more like a nightmare than a joke, I assure you. They were convinced that we were American spies, and none of us spoke enough Arabic to persuade them otherwise. So they marched us a hundred and fifty miles to their headquarters, near the coast, and sent a demand for a million dollars to the American

Embassy at Sahma.'

'What happened?' she couldn't stop herself from asking.

'The Americans said it was none of their business, naturally. They had enough problems of their own just then. But somehow Peter got to hear of it. He felt it was his responsibility to pull his fellow Brits out of the fire. He travelled overland in a Bedford truck to negotiate for our release with the guerrillas. Since the Emir was on what amounted to a war footing with his neighbours, Peter took a considerable risk in doing so. What was even more remarkable,' Adam smiled tautly, 'Peter managed to get the Emir himself to pay our ransom. Persuaded him it was in the interests of the harmony of the whole region, and the international prestige of the Emir personally.' He stretched, as though his powerful muscles were cramped. 'It wasn't the kind of thing you could forget in a hurry. After that, we became friends. I came to rely on your father's advice. He always had the right information, the right judgement. But I was never able to pay that debt back before he died. Not fully.'

'And now you're going to repay that debt?' Margot threw at him tensely. 'Using me to soothe your unsettled conscience?'

'If you want to see it like that,' he replied with unruffled calm. 'What's eating you?'

'Nothing's eating me.' She was unused to wine, and the claret had made her head swim slightly. What he'd just told her had unleashed a wave of conflicting emotions in her. Pride for her father, yes, concern for Adam's life, too. But above all, a sense of disappointment that was dagger-sharp in its intensity.

It had all been for Peter's sake.

All this kindness, all this tenderness, this whole elaborate charade—it had all been designed to pay off a debt to her father. Not for Margot. For Peter.

From now on, she would have to keep reminding herself that she wasn't here out of any personal merit. She was only here because of her father, and if Adam was kind to her, or harsh with her, or twisted her poor heart round his little finger—it was all because of something her father had done.

A guest on sufferance. Not here on her own account, but because of someone else.

'Quite a story,' she said drily, not meeting his enquiring eyes. 'I presume you feel you're quits with my father, now?'

'It's not a question of that,' he replied coolly. 'It's never been as simple as that, Margot. Your recovery delights me, but it doesn't cancel my debt to your father. I remember once telling you that I was doing this for your sake, Margot.'

'Not for my father's?'

'Only very indirectly.' He pointed at her plate. 'Stop asking so many questions.'

'But what exactly do you mean, for *my* sake?' She was tight-lipped. 'I don't understand what that means.'

'And I don't understand why you're making such a point of it,' he said warily.

'Has it ever occurred to you that I might have some feelings of my own?' Margot tried to keep her voice light, though her feelings were rising dangerously. He was avoiding the real question, and they both knew it. 'That I might want you to care for me for my own sake, and not just because of something my father did six years ago?'

'Margot,' he said gently, 'I've said it twice already. Your welfare is very important to me.'

'My *welfare*,' she repeated tautly. 'That has a very impersonal ring. Like a teacher, or a social worker talking.'

'I don't feel like a teacher or a social worker,' he said patiently. 'I only meant to express my concern. Not to patronise.'

'And what if I need more than your concern?' she demanded, unable to keep her words under control any longer. 'Now that I'm free of the addiction, your debt will be discharged, won't it? You'll want to pack me off to a nice new job somewhere, and feel your conscience greatly eased. Isn't that right?'

He hadn't touched his food. 'You're being unfair,' he said quietly. 'You're overtired.'

'Maybe I am,' she said fiercely, fighting down the prickle of tears in her eyes. 'But in case what happened out there in the river tonight has slipped your mind, I've become rather attached to you lately!'

He stared at her in silence, tiny flames from the candles reflected in each eye. She regretted the words the minute they were spoken. She'd just broken one of her own cardinal rules—never show anyone your true feelings about them.

'I'm sorry,' she said, with a breathless, painful laugh. 'I should never have said that.'

'It's better said than unsaid.' He tossed his napkin in a crumpled heap on to the table and rose, holding out his hand to her, eyes serious. 'Let's sit by the fire, Margot. I want to talk to you.'

Her heart was thudding dully as they sat together in the

warmth of the fire. The two carved polar bears snarled silently at her, reminding her of that first night in this cottage.

'I think I know what you're going to say,' she said unhappily. 'But go ahead, all the same.'

'I intend to.' His voice was gentle, but there was little warmth in it. The masculine planes of his face were almost harsh now. 'You must understand how inevitable your feelings are, Margot. You've just been through a crucially important experience. In the past few weeks you've changed from an addict into a healthy, beautiful woman with all her life before her. You're ready for love, I understand that even better than you yourself do——'

'But not with you,' she said, looking up with a painful smile.

'For one thing, I'm more than ten years older than you are.' His eyes were cool, emotionless. 'For another, I would be taking advantage of you in a very ugly way.'

'Why?' she demanded urgently.

'Don't be silly,' he reproved. 'You must surely understand that all your feelings towards me have become very exaggerated, pearl. We've been locked up together for weeks, in a particularly intimate and emotional situation.' He smiled with a hint of tiredness. 'A few weeks from now, when you've got your life together again, you'll see me in perspective. I hope you'll always see me as an old friend, but I know you won't see me as anything more than that.'

'An old friend,' she echoed, tasting the emptiness in the phrase. 'You mean I don't know what I'm talking about? I'm too mixed up to know whether what I feel for you is real—or just infatuation?'

'Yes,' he said flatly. 'That *is* what I mean. You've been badly hurt in your short life, Margot. I don't think I could take the risk of hurting you any further.' His voice was firm. 'Not ever.'

'And if it weren't for that?' she asked tensely. 'If we'd just met at a nightclub or in a park—how would you feel about me then?'

'There's no point in pursuing hypothetical speculations,' he retorted. 'We're talking about you and me, the way we are.'

'No, we're not,' she said bitterly. 'You keep avoiding *me*. Whatever you do is always for some high motive, for my dead father, or because you don't want to take advantage of me, whatever that means——' She drew a shaky breath, her eyes dark with emotion. 'Can't you understand how that hurts? Adam, my whole life long I've been aching for someone to care for me for my own sake. I'm not asking you to love me——'

'Then what *are* you asking?' he demanded as her words petered out. 'Do you simply want to transfer your addiction from heroin to me?'

'That's cruel,' she said quietly. 'I'm just asking you not to hold back. That if there *is* any emotion in you, you don't hide it behind a screen of fine moral principles.'

'You tend to undervalue fine moral principles,' Adam said drily. 'Sometimes, they matter more than all the raw emotion in the world.'

'At this stage of my life,' said Margot unsteadily, 'raw emotion happens to be what I need to stay alive. And I'm not being melodramatic, Adam. I'm in a vacuum. I never know whether a given word, a given kiss, is meant for *me*—or just done out of your natural generosity.' She closed her eyes with a trembling laugh. 'Oh, you're generous. A good man, the best I've known. But you can't treat me with your gloves on twenty-four hours a day. I don't mind if there's nothing there—just as long as I know how you feel.'

'All right.' There was the smoky hint of a challenge in his smile. 'I do care. Are you satisfied now?'

'Then hold me.' She shook her head as she saw his expression change. 'I'm not trying to bribe you this time. I just want you to hold me.'

The leopard's eyes seemed to flare for a moment, then softened into gentleness. He reached for her, cradling her in strong arms.

She sighed shakily as she laid her cheek against his broad shoulder. 'I need you so much,' she whispered, not sure if he could even hear her. 'You're everything to me, Adam ...'

He took her face in his hands, and kissed her parted lips. The touch of his mouth was as heady as wine, making her senses swim. She felt almost afraid suddenly, her body as shivery as it had been that first night in the cottage.

'You're trembling like a netted bird,' he muttered huskily. 'Do I frighten you?'

'You terrify me,' she said softly. He kissed her again, more fiercely now, his hands sliding across the naked skin of her back under the sweater, his tongue probing the inner sweetness of her mouth as the passion flared between them like flame licking across spilled petrol.

'*No!*' He drew back, his voice unsteady. 'I mean what I say, Margot.' Strong fingers prised her hands loose from around his neck. 'God damn it, can't you learn to protect yourself?'

'Do I need to protect myself from you, Adam?' she whispered, looking up at him with cloudy eyes, her moist lips parted.

'Don't look at me like that,' he said, almost savagely. He walked to the window, thrusting his hands deep into his pockets and stared out into the darkness beyond. 'I might have known,' he said harshly, almost to himself. 'I might have known what would happen to us.' When he turned to her, his face was set and grim. 'You're practically recovered, Margot. I'm beginning to feel that the sooner you get back to your old life, and out of mine, the better it will be for both of us.'

Margot had expected Adam to be cool with her the next day, and he was little more than polite. She wasn't feeling exactly joyous herself. The pain of having made a complete fool of herself was acute. Why hadn't she kept her mouth shut last night—would she never learn?

He had to be up at the stud that morning, to meet some prospective clients, and his invitation to accompany him was more like an order.

'I've arranged for David to saddle up Aspic for you this morning,' he said over breakfast. 'That's if you want to ride?'

'Thanks,' she said with an attempt at a smile. 'But you don't have to entertain me, Adam.'

'You're showing promise,' he said matter-of-factly. 'You're good with horses. You should keep up your riding when you get back to London.'

It was said deliberately, she knew that. Not to hurt, just to prepare her for the end of this idyll. But the words wounded, made her wince despite her resolve not to burden him with any more emotional displays.

She dressed in a denim skirt and a cotton check blouse, an outfit that was in almost exact counterpoint to the deep blue jeans and the faded shirt which hugged the muscular shape of his chest.

'I haven't had my hair done in weeks,' she muttered, more to herself than to him as she checked herself in the hall mirror. 'I look a mess.'

'I like your hair like that.' She met his dark gaze in the mirror. 'Beautiful hair doesn't need expensive treatment,' he commented, and walked out to the car.

'Beautiful hair doesn't need expensive treatment,' she told her reflection in the mirror, shrugged, and followed him out.

'I'll show you round the Hall when I've finished,' he offered as they drove through the archway. She nodded her thanks, and he glanced at her. 'You feeling all right?'

'Fine,' she said flatly.

'This will take about an hour, pearl. I'll come and find you in the paddock.'

She nodded again.

It was very cold. Though it was early morning, the sun was low, and the trees cast long shadows across the fallow fields. Absently, Margot watched their own attenuated shadows as they walked across the yard, two tall figures, not holding hands. Two separate people, bound only by the coincidence of travelling in the same direction.

As she hoisted herself on to the mare's back, tears were very close behind her eyes. What expectations could she possibly have of Adam? He obviously didn't have any confidence in her, after all. He would never be able to trust her and respect her the way she needed him to.

She should never have told him about those inner
feelings. She would have been far wiser to have kept them
in.

Under David's watchful eye, she cantered Aspic across
the grass, wondering how she was ever going to survive
without Adam ...

'The Harcourt family, who'd owned it for generations,
died out fifty years ago.' Adam was leading her up the
marble staircase and through the main door of the house,
an hour or so later. 'The stud was kept ticking over by the
farmer who bought it from them, using only about a tenth
of the capacity of the place. But the house itself had stood
empty, and it was badly run down, on the brink of being
demolished by the executors.'

'No!' Margot exclaimed, marvelling at the perfection of
the lovely old façade. 'Who could destroy something like
this?'

'That's the way I felt,' Adam smiled. His eyes were
drifting over her figure, pausing at the swell of her breasts
against the cotton of her shirt. 'You're putting on weight,'
he said softly.

'Am I getting too fat?' she asked with an anxious glance
at herself.

'I didn't say that.' He pulled his gaze away from her, as
if with an effort, and turned. 'Come.'

Beyond the vestibule, the great house was more or less
bare. The silence was immense in the high-vaulted
interior, and the black cables of power equipment snaked
in every direction across the gleaming, bare, beechwood
floor.

'There's not much more to do now,' Adam told her as

they walked through. 'But it's taken a monumental effort to save the old place. So far I've spent probably twice what the place is worth.' He didn't look particularly perturbed about the obviously huge expense.

Over the serpentine fireplace hung a vast oil painting, almost half life-size, of a black stallion; the house in the background was clearly Harcourt Hall.

'Macallen?' queried Margot, and he nodded.

'The ground floor restoration is finished,' he told her, his deep voice echoing. He watched the expression of wide-eyed wonder on her upturned face. 'So's the second floor. With luck, the top floor will be ready by next March.'

She digested that in silence, and followed him through the exquisite, empty rooms. Everywhere, the same beautiful blondewood floors gleamed. Many of the rooms were panelled in oak and mahogany to their stuccoed ceilings, while some had obviously been freshly decorated. Here and there a vast canvas hung over a stone fireplace, but for the most part the immaculate walls were as bare as the floors. 'It's stunning,' she breathed.

Again, his eyes were on her. 'You like it?'

'I love it.'

He reach out to give her cheek the barest caress, then thrust his hands into his pockets. 'When I bought the estate, a huge quantity of antiques and paintings were still in the house.' He looked around the bare walls with intent grey eyes. 'Some of it was rubbish, or ruined, but a lot wasn't. Most of it's in storage in the cellars, waiting for the house to be ready. The rest of it, the really beautiful things, are being restored.'

'It's going to be an overwhelming place,' Margot said

dreamily. 'This is the kind of house most people just dream of . . .'

'It's a home,' he said gently. 'It always has been. And while I'm alive, it always will be. That sculpture is by Marise Vladek,' he added as they walked into the next room. She followed his eyes. In the big bay window, a bronze mare and foal stood in perfect harmony, outlined by sunlight. The artist had captured the gentle protective-ness of the mare, and the gangly grace of the foal, with almost magical skill.

'It's a lovely thing,' she said softly, stroking the cool bronze of the sculpture. She was oddly moved by his choice of the piece. Instinctively, she knew it reflected more than just Adam's love of horses. It reflected his own desire to make Harcourt a home. A home, with a family in it, full of laughter and joy. What woman would create it with him, share it with him?

He led her through to one of the high bay windows on the east side. 'The Hall always was a centre for good horses. Harcourt once produced some of England's best racehorses. I intend to make sure it more than lives up to its tradition.'

She stared out. A string of glossy horses was moving across the close-shorn autumn field, the diminutive stable lads muffled against the cold. Adam came to lean on the sill beside her, the momentary touch of his body reminding her painfully of last night.

'That's Spindrift,' he said, nodding at the leading animal. 'His juvenile fillies are among the best in the country. One of his colts was sold in Kentucky earlier this year for two and a half million dollars.'

'Wow!' Margot exclaimed in awe. There was pride in

Adam's face, but she knew intinctively that it wasn't the money he felt passion for. It was the quality of breeding that could command such sums.

She glanced up into the golden face, aching for him with all her heart. 'You really love horses, don't you?'

'Yes.'

'More than you could love—a woman?' she asked hesitantly.

'That's a typical woman's question. It's a different thing, pearl.' Adam folded his arms, looking down at the field with brooding eyes. 'Horses are my life's work. They don't compete with my love-life.' He paused to watch a bay mare canter up to the fence, steam pluming up from her mouth. 'Look at that mare. I bred her, five years ago. We broke her ourselves, as a yearling, and raced her in the Korda colours. I watched her grow into an outstanding performer, saw her win race after race. Now she's back here at Harcourt, come full cycle. I want to see her foals repeat the performance, Margot. That's what I do it for. For the satisfaction it brings me.' He glanced at Margot who was watching the flawless beauty of the animals in silence. 'The woman I eventually marry will never have to vie with my work. But she'd have to understand what my work means to me.'

He led her upstairs. The clean smells of paint and varnish were in the air as they mounted the main staircase. It, too, had been newly built out of mahogany, and with a sense of awe Margot tried to calculate the thousands he must have spent on this house. Hundreds of thousands. Adam Korda had achieved a wealth and power that few men dreamed of.

One of the massive bedrooms on the first floor had

already been furnished. 'This is my room,' he said, in answer to her enquiring expression. 'I sometimes sleep here.'

She walked in slowly, the dove-grey carpet soft underfoot. The four-poster bed, with its magnificent turned newels, was flanked by two big paintings of female nudes. The rest of the bedroom furniture was heavy and masculine, but obviously very valuable. The Slavic decoration suggested family heirlooms.

She looked at the bed. On the wine-red coverlet, their bodies would look exquisite, dramatically erotic. She closed her eyes for a moment, feeling desire and sadness mingling inside her into an emotion she could not name.

Adam moved to a writing table by the window, and pulled open a drawer. 'This is for you.'

She took the photograph. It was a colour shot of two men at a restaurant table, laughing. Her father and Adam. The bottles of wine on the table indicated a festive meal in progress.

She stared at the photograph, seeing the obvious affection between the two men. She could almost hear that laugh of her father's, hearty and booming. A sense of fresh grief rose in her for a moment. Such a waste, so many lost chances.

'That was taken two years ago,' Adam told her. 'A birthday party.'

'I don't have very many pictures of him,' she said sorrowfully.

'Nor do I. It never seemed important at the time. It never does. We spoke about you a lot that day.'

Her eyes were wet now. 'I—I'm sorry,' she said in a choked voice. 'I don't—seem to have—a handkerchief.'

'Here.' He passed her one, and she tried to stem the tears, gulping back the sobs. 'Sit down for a moment.' She sank on to the bed obediently. Adam sat beside her and slid his arm comfortingly round her shoulders. She laid her head against him, sighing raggedly.

'I've got one real regret,' she said in a low voice. 'That I never got a chance to tell him how sorry I was before he died. About the way I'd behaved, I mean.'

'I think your father understood you better than you think,' Adam smiled. 'He always had faith in you, pearl.'

You're not as unlike me as you imagine, Margot.

She shook the memory away. 'Sorry to go all mushy,' she apologised, drying her eyes. She looked up into his face. 'I'd made a resolution not to be so feeble, too!'

'You're not feeble,' he said softly. Their eyes met, and Margot felt something stir in her heart, knew it was also stirring in his. 'God,' he whispered, almost to himself, 'you're becoming so beautiful, Margot. Every day you seem to be opening, like a flower.'

Their kiss was as gentle as thistledown. He cupped her face in his hands, his mouth caressing hers with infinite tenderness, then slowly drew her back to lie facing him on the red coverlet.

'What are you doing to me?' he whispered. 'You bewitch me, pearl . . .'

Under her timid hands, his body was hard with power, the muscles taut with the promise of passion. And she was melting into his arms, her mouth parting helplessly for his kiss. She clung to him with trembling eagerness, her need for him flooding her, driving out every emotion but her need to be fulfilled by his love.

The silence of the great house fell around them,

peaceful and loving.

His mouth was both hungry and generous. He used it to tease her at first, kissing her eyelids, her temples, her throat, the exquisite line of her collarbones; and then, as he impatiently unfastened her blouse, the scented valley between her breasts. There were no reins on their passion now. Margot knotted her fingers in his dark, springy hair as he cupped her breasts in his hands, his tongue and lips firming each nipple into a concentrated peak of desire.

'God, you're so lovely,' he said huskily, staring at her slender body. 'Lovelier than any porcelain.'

'And you're magnificent,' Margot whispered softly, her arms twining around his neck as her eyes became dark, passionate slits.

He smiled down at her, his face smoky with desire. 'Do I still terrify you?'

'More than ever!' She wanted him with an ache that was becoming unbearable. Why did a woman always have to hold back? Was it all part of the pleasure of love to be forced to wait, attend on the will of the man? Or was he used to sophisticated, liberated, aggressive lovers . . .?

Damn those other women. *Damn* them. As though wanting to crush their memory away for ever, she kissed his face, his throat, the smooth skin of his shoulders, hungering for the musky smell of his body.

He pulled his shirt impatiently off, and she reached out to touch the beautiful nakedness of his torso. She'd wanted to touch him like this for so long. To run her palms over the powerful muscles of his chest, to feel the hard points of his man's nipples stiffening under her touch. To caress the line of his neck where his muscular throat joined the arching wings of his collarbones, where the crisp hair started, and curled like something alive, down to his loins. Under the warm skin, his heart was pounding like an engine, making something seem to melt inside her . . .

Urgent, yet never rough, Adam's fingers tugged the waistband of her skirt open, trailed the zip down with wicked expertise, then drifted across her loins and the satin skin of her thighs.

She whispered his name unsteadily as his caress reached the taut black silk of her briefs. She'd never felt anything like this sweet agony before. She moaned softly as his hand cupped the mound of her sex possessively, a caress that was both protective and achingly sexual.

'Adam, my love . . .' An ecstasy of giddiness washed over her as his fingers moved beneath the flimsy material to touch her melting womanhood. Her own hands were timidly seeking the hot centre of his manhood, making him groan with pleasure, His sexuality was unashamed, arrogant and proud in its strength.

'When you touch me like that, I could die,' he said huskily. He drew back, but only to remove the rest of his clothes, and then to undress her, with slow, lingering delight, kissing each new sweet stretch of skin as it was revealed.

'I've wanted you since that first night,' he said gently, his lips warm against her hip. 'When you had that nightmare, and I got into bed beside you. I've never wanted a woman as much as I wanted you then.'

'You s-seemed so much in control, then,' she whispered, her fingers trailing through his hair.

The first urgency of their need had given way to a steady flame that burned with ever-brighter, ever-warmer intensity. Their naked bodies had a music of their

own, a music that began with single notes, dropping into
the stillness of the night like pebbles into still water.
Touches, kisses, caresses, a pattern of love that began to
fuse into a symphony.

It was as though he wanted to taste every inch of her,
prolonging their lovemaking almost unbearably. He was
lifting her higher all the time, stretching her passion like a
bow until she thought she couldn't wait a moment longer.
His kiss was shamelessly erotic, his mouth adoring her
thighs, the secret sweetness of her loins, his tongue finding
the aching centre of her need. Pleasure peaked unbearably in her, her moan telling him how ready she was. And
when at last he came to her, whispering her name, she
arched her body to his, her thighs parting to hold his hard
flanks as their lips met.

He entered her with slow, possessive force, making her
gasp helplessly. He was so big, thrusting so deep into her
body, his manhood filling her utterly. It was almost as
though her body were too small at first, as though they
were mismatched; but his lovemaking was overwhelm-
ingly gentle, his arms holding her tight against him as he
used his potency with gradual, controlled power to flood
her with a swelling pleasure that grew until she clenched
her fingers in his thick hair, as though clinging to the
mane of a runaway stallion, urging him to hold nothing
back.

Her eyes were closed, his mouth roaming hotly across
her face, his husky whisper telling her she maddened him,
calling her beautiful, telling her things about her body
that would once have made her blush in horror, but which
now exalted her shamelessly ...

She cried out as the passion took her in a grasp she

couldn't escape. She had a fleeting moment of terror that she would spoil this magnificent magic between them; but as she arched helplessly in the completion of her own act of love, her body compelled his to respond, and he became hers as he called out her name, crushing her to him.

For a compressed eternity, the world stopped turning, and every star in the heavens was stilled for them. Then the drugged pleasure of satiety filled her veins, relaxing every inch of her.

She was whispering his name long afterwards, as she sank into sleep in his arms, and the world slowly began to turn again.

'Adam . . .'

'I'm here.'

She drifted into sleep, knowing with awe and wonder and fulfilment that she was in love.

She woke first, her head pillowed on the tanned skin of his chest. Gently, so as not to wake him, she raised herself on one elbow, and looked down at his tranquil face. In sleep, he was as beautiful as an angel. Her angel. With the utmost delicacy, she traced the chiselled line of his nose and lips with her fingertips, adoring him.

The throbbing in her loins reminded her intensely of the sensation of him inside her, the way he'd crushed her in his arms, the dizzying things he'd said to her . . .

It was late afternoon, a great splash of sunlight glowing on the deep red wallpaper of the bedroom. Time had ceased to matter, though. She and Adam were caught in a well of stillness that had no dimensions except their own.

She would never forget this afternoon. Not just the physical ecstasy of their lovemaking, but the almost mystical sense of union she'd had with Adam. Nothing could ever take that away from her.

He stirred slightly against her, the brush of their naked skins awakening him, and his eyes opened to dark slits.

'Hello,' she whispered, and bent to kiss him with clinging lips.

'Hello, pearl.' Adam's voice was husky. He reached up to touch her face. 'How do you feel?'

'If I could tell you,' she smiled. 'I would.'

He didn't answer her smile, just stared searchingly into her face, as though gazing into the deep waters of a well. 'You know that this is the end,' he said gently. 'Don't you?'

'It's just the beginning,' she contradicted him, shaking her head.

'No.' Adam rolled to the side of the bed, and reached for his denims, 'It should never have happened.'

'There was no way it couldn't have happened, Adam.' Margot's face was tender, vulnerable. 'We've both been waiting for it. At least, I know I have. All my life.'

'Damn,' he whispered, turning to look at her over his broad shoulder. 'What crazy urge makes you say things like that?'

'If what I feel now is crazy,' she smiled sadly, 'then I don't ever want to be sane.'

'It's time you started your life again. You're going back to London,' he said with quiet determination. 'Tomorrow.'

The words didn't shock her. They hurt, but she'd been expecting them, somehow. 'Why?' she asked him in a small voice, hugging her naked breasts.

'Because there's nothing more I can do for you. From here on you have to start making your own way.' He rose fluidly to his feet, buttoning the jeans across his lean waist.

'Adam——' she pleaded, but he laid his fingers on her lips to silence her.

'Hush, pearl. I never meant this to happen. It can only end in disaster—for me, but most of all for you.' He turned away, mouth slanting in self-condemnation. 'And having proved that I can't control myself where you're concerned,' he went on harshly as he reached for his shirt, 'I think that the best thing is for us to separate as quickly and cleanly as possible.'

She felt anguish tighten every nerve in her body. 'How will I survive without you?' she asked him painfully.

'That's one of the questions you're going to have to answer for yourself.' She watched the muscles ripple under his tanned skin as he hauled the cotton over his head. Adam pulled the shirt straight over his hard flanks. 'What I've done already is bad enough. I don't want a love affair with you, Margot.' Deep and calm, his eyes met hers. 'I'm sorry, pearl,' he said quietly.

'I'm sorry, too.' She looked down, her eyes blinded with sudden tears. She was sorrier than she'd ever been. Sorry because she knew he was wrong. Sick and sad and sorry because she knew he would never change his mind about her. 'Why can't you give us a chance?' she pleaded without hope. 'Why can't you admit the possibility that you might be mistaken, that maybe I *do* love you? That maybe I'd have loved you wherever and however and whenever we'd met?'

'And why can't you grow up?' he demanded, almost

savagely. 'You don't love me—you're grateful to me. There's no other basis for a relationship, Margot.' He lifted his watch off the bedside table, the diamonds sparkling in the sun, and fastened it around his wrist. 'Don't confuse gratitude with love, girl. That's the oldest mistake in the book.'

'Why are you being so brutal about this?' she asked tightly, staring up at the handsome face.

'I'm simply trying to bring you back down to earth,' he replied grimly. 'Just lately you've had too many stars in your eyes to see anything clearly.'

'I see,' Margot retorted with a flash of bitterness. 'Who the hell do you think put those stars in my eyes in the first place, Adam?'

'Don't blame me for your own illusions.' There was no warmth at all in the grey eyes now. 'I warned you as clearly as I could.'

'My love for you is no illusion!'

Patience wore thin in his expression. 'You've chosen to fill your head with romantic pink clouds, Margot. That's an illusion.'

'Is it?' She tried to keep the emotion out of her voice, not wanting to let him see how much she was hurting. 'And does this afternoon also come under the heading of illusory pink clouds?'

'I think the wisest course would be to forget all about this afternoon,' he said, the temperature of his voice Arctic. 'Permanently.'

'That's not going to be as easy as you make it sound!' she challenged, overlaying her pain with heavy irony. 'Our lovemaking was real, at any rate. Funny, I thought people had to be in love before sex became that good.' Her mouth twisted in a humourless smile. 'Or did you have stars in your eyes, too?'

His face closed like a door being slammed. 'I was a fool,' he said sharply. 'But I've had the sense to recognise my own folly.'

'Are you telling me our lovemaking meant nothing?' she asked shakily.

His lip curled. 'This is the twentieth century, Margot. When a man makes love to a woman, it doesn't necessarily imply a permanent relationship.'

'I'm not as naïve as all that,' she retorted. 'But I've been labouring under the delusion that this afternoon was something special. Not just casual sex between casual strangers.' Her mouth curved with passion. 'Maybe I was wrong.'

'There's no *maybe* about it.'

She swung herself out of bed in silence. As she moved, she could feel the sweet bruise of his lovemaking inside her, and now the ache intensified unbearably.

The sense of foreboding that had been lurking at the back of her mind for weeks had suddenly taken on a dark form. Reality had cut into the delicious warmth of her emotions like a winter wind slashing down tender seedlings. Margot had no illusions that this was not the end. She knew the strength of Adam's will well enough to understand that he meant every word he said.

Mornings after could be so very cruel. How many times had she had to learn that simple fact in the course of her life? It was time to pay the price for what she'd taken from him.

'It seems I've been mistaken about you,' she said shortly. The glitter in his eyes was like the turning of a blade in the sun, but his voice stayed smoky-smooth. 'It seems you have. I'd rather you thought anything about me than wasted energy imagining some romantic nonsense that could never come true.'

'Oh, don't worry,' she gritted, 'I'm long past any romantic nonsense, Adam. You might find I can be every bit as hard as you can.' She drew a shaky breath to try and steady her emotions. It hurt too much to quarrel with Adam, and now she just wanted to get over the pain ahead of her as quickly as possible. 'At least you've been honest. I never knew how you really felt until now.'

He walked back to her, hands thrust into his pockets so that his jeans were stretched taut across his hips and thighs. 'You've got your own way to make, now, pearl.' His gaze held her eyes relentlessly. 'Forget about me. You don't need additional burdens like love at this stage. You need to set your sights on getting your life straight, with no distractions, no side issues. There's a lot on your plate, girl. Finding a new job. Making it up with your mother and her husband. Getting back into a useful, fulfilled life. Spreading your wings.' He grimaced at her expression. 'You didn't think this could last for ever, did you?'

'I wish it could,' she choked. 'I don't want anything else, Adam. I never will.'

He laughed softly. 'You don't even know how many wonderful things there are in the world to want, pearl.'

She was crying now, but he didn't comfort her. 'Will I—will I ever see you again?' she asked tearfully.

'When you don't need to see me,' he said gently. 'Maybe. When you've stopped needing me.'

'That'll be never!'

'It'll be soon.'

'Oh, Adam,' she sobbed, 'I feel so lost . . .'

'You're not lost,' he contradicted her briskly. 'You're on the right track, now. You'll never go back to drugs, we both know that. From now on, things will go right for you, instead of wrong all the time.'

She pressed her hands to her breaking heart.

'Come on, pearl,' he said. He put his arm round her shoulders, and walked with her to the window. The primeval mass of Darkrising Woods spread out before them. 'The woods are lovely, dark, and deep,' he quoted softly. 'But you have promises to keep. And miles to go before you sleep.'

CHAPTER EIGHT

EDDIE GRANT lunged after the ball, just managed to get his racket to it, and set Margot up for an easy kill. She slammed the little black ball into the far corner of the squash court with a certain inner satisfaction.

Eddie didn't even bother to go for it. He trotted for his kit, panting, and mopped his sweaty face.

'Damn,' he complained, mouth muffled by the Lancaster Club towel. 'I'm exhausted. You're too fit, Prescott.'

'It's just an eye for the ball,' she said smugly, bouncing the racket off the heel of her hand. She was out of breath, but not much, and she wasn't altogether joking when she offered, 'Care for another game? We've still got the court for fifteen minutes.'

Eddie glanced at Margot, taking in her long, slim legs and immaculately unruffled white skirt. 'Thanks, but no thanks,' he said drily. 'My ego's taken enough of a pounding this morning.'

'It's these debauched weekends of yours,' she accused him, walking across to her kitbag. 'Every Monday I thrash you, and every Thursday you thrash me.'

'You try too hard. Why aren't you one of these diplomatic women who always let the man win?' he sighed, mopping the bald patch at the top of his head as they walked to the exit. At thirty-two, he was already losing his fine black hair, and was very sensitive about it. He always wore tinted glasses which, together with his drooping moustache, gave him a slightly sinister air which

146

he thought compensated for the hair loss.

'Because I need the exercise,' she answered his question. Heads were turning as they walked along the plant-lined gallery. Men always stared at Margot at the Lancaster, their gaze usually first attracted by those long, dancer's legs, then held by the sweet, oval face that was framed by hair as black and glossy as a jackdaw's wing. She smiled at someone who'd waved at her, but it wasn't a smile that gave much away. Her Mona Lisa smile, Eddie called it. Fleeting, holding some sad mystery you couldn't quite grasp at.

'Meet you in the restaurant afterwards,' Eddie invited as they split up to go to their respective showers, and Margot nodded acquiescence.

She liked the Lancaster Club. Membership was expensive, but the Committee offered special rates to the newspaper she was now on, and it had the sort of facilities that made most other sports clubs look second-rate.

As she soaped herself in the cubicle, she was thinking of Adam. Which wasn't unusual. Not a day of the past four months had gone by without her thinking of Adam. Sometimes the memories made her dreamy-eyed. Sometimes they brought the quick tears to her eyes.

And sometimes, as now, while she rinsed the shampoo away, they curved the soft arc of her lips into a smile of pure pleasure. She was thinking of the evening she had fallen in the river, of how they'd kissed in midstream, her wet face pressed to his, his hands buried in the tangle of her hair.

She felt the old, familiar ache spreading through her, and squeezed her eyes shut as she held her face up to the spray. This was her favourite fantasy. That Adam would step into the shower, as naked as she was, hands reaching possessively to hold her breasts as his mouth sought hers . . .

But it didn't happen. She stepped out, dripping, long black hair clinging to the superb lines of her temples and cheeks, and pulled her towel off the rack.

The pair of middle-class, middle-aged women who were chatting at the basin both turned to give Margot's figure glances that were that uniquely female mixture of admiration and envy.

Slender as a ballet dancer with firm, high breasts and tautly muscled thighs, Margot Prescott was as close to physical perfection as she would ever be. The years would deepen her beauty, fill out the curves of breasts and hips, but they could add nothing to the grace she'd been born to fulfil.

The two women waited until she'd slipped on her bra and panties before one cleared her throat lightly.

'I read your article in *Liberty*.' Margot looked up, and the woman smiled timidly. 'It is Margot Prescott, isn't it? I read your article in *Liberty*, about drug addiction. It was very good.'

'Thank you,' Margot nodded, towelling her hair dry. But the woman, who had worried blue eyes and untidy, mouse-coloured hair, wasn't finished.

'You seemed to *understand* everything. Almost as though you'd been an addict yourself.'

'Which is ridiculous,' her smarter and younger friend put in with a smile, looking at Margot's healthy body, the tan of her skin emphasised by her delicate cream lingerie.

'It struck a chord,' the first woman went on. Both were in designer tracksuits, and holding rackets, but Margot had the feeling they weren't here for sporting reasons. She smiled, and glanced longingly at the row of hairdryers on the opposite wall. She and Eddie had to be back at the office by two. 'It's my daughter, you see.' The mousy woman suddenly looked as though she was going to cry. 'I mean, I *know* she's using drugs, but when I try to confront her with it, she just lies and lies . . .'

'Just as well we finished fifteen minutes early,' grumbled Eddie as Margot hastened into the restuarant a quarter of an hour later. 'What kept you? New hairstyle?'

'Does it look like it?' Margot grimaced. Her hair was still only half dry, because she'd never got to that hairdryer. 'I got caught up in conversation with someone in the changing-rooms, and couldn't get away.'

'Women!' Eddie sighed as they moved towards the buffet, collecting trays en route.

Poor mousy lady, Margot thought sadly. She'd given her the best advice she could, had passed on the addresses of organisations that would help, but the outlook was grimly uncertain. If only every addicted girl had an Adam Korda to haul her, kicking and screaming, out of the whirlpool . . .

'Hoi, dreamy! Want a beer?'

'I'll stick to fresh orange,' she decided, hunting for one that wasn't a seething mass of preservatives and colourants.

'There are limits to which any human being can take health, Prescott.' Eddie watched with disapproval as she chose a green salad while his own plate was being loaded with french fries. 'Don't you have *any* vices at all?'

'I just don't see the point of killing yourself on a squash court for an hour,' she smiled, 'then loading up on carbohydrates. You're getting a pot belly.' She took pity on his anguished look. 'A pot tummy, then. You ought to eat more salads.'

'You're a real ego-booster this morning,' he muttered. 'OK, pass me one of those tomato things.'

She didn't let him pay at the till, even though he tried to make quite a point of it. Her relationship with Eddie Grant, who'd been divorced for three years, was undefined, and that was the way she wanted it to stay. Eddie was good-looking in an earnest way, and was an excellent journalist. In that he took her out to dinner or the pictures regularly, and played squash with her twice a week, he qualified as her current male friend. And Eddie's presence kept other men in the office from bothering with her.

But she'd made it very clear that their friendship didn't include sex. And she always paid her own way.

But despite the fact that Eddie insisted on calling her by her surname, as though she were some hard-nosed feminist, he had a very soft centre; and she'd seen in his brown eyes more than once recently that he was building up a substantial crush on her.

Soon, she knew that he would make a really determined effort to bed her. She would repulse him equally determinedly. And Eddie would probably walk out of the relationship at that point, in a cloud of incomprehension and wounded male pride, and she would have to look for a new squash partner. She didn't look forward to what she foresaw with any pleasure. But nor did she kid herself that she would feel any real regret when it happened.

After Adam, no man would ever mean anything to her. There was simply no one who would ever measure up to him, no one who would ever remotely touch the places in her that he'd touched, that he continued, every hour of every day, to touch. She was Adam's, in her heart, even though she'd lost him for ever. And no one could ever possess her again, not even temporarily.

Eddie sank half his beer with a noise like a very dry desert absorbing a cloudburst. 'What's on the agenda?'

'This afternoon? I've got to get that review on to Lawrence's desk by four.'

'Nice for some,' he sniffed. 'Listening to pop records and getting paid for it. Not what *I* call journalism. You're not on *City News* now, Prescott.'

'Contemporary jazz-rock, not pop,' she corrected him, tucking into her cold meats and salad. 'And considering it's a look-back over the past three years, there's been a lot more involved than just listening to records!'

'You weren't even born three years ago,' he grinned. 'Editor's pet! You can't tell me that the contemporary music review isn't just about the cushiest column going. Apart from the good food guide, of course, and that wobbly old codger who writes about wine.'

'It has its compensations,' she conceded. The *London Herald* was a notoriously conservative newspaper. Some of the staff had never recovered from the shock of having pictures on the front page—let alone the fact that an attractive female journalist called Margot Prescott, formerly of *City News*, had been employed to cover contemporary youth culture.

Most of the rest, however, including Eddie—despite his teasing—recognised the wisdom of an editor who was angling for an increasingly younger market. 'If you want them to read the *Herald* in their forties, fifties, and sixties,' Lawrence Sweetney was on record as saying, 'you've got to get them in their twenties and thirties.'

It had been the heroin article, published in the women's magazine *Liberty*, which had decided Sweetney that he wanted Margot for the *Herald*.

She'd written the story in that first unbelievably painful week after she'd left Harcourt, and it had carried a blazing conviction that had attracted a lot of very favourable attention. The pain she'd gone through during those first days was something she could never reveal to anyone. It was there, in the article, but only she knew that. She'd never re-read the article, not wanting to bring any of that pain back into the calm that she'd managed to surround herself with.

That calm, that Mona Lisa smile, was the result of hard, cruel effort. She'd had to pull her life together by its ragged edges, fashion a new existence that didn't have Adam Korda as its centre. Hard, cruel, bitter effort. More painful than giving up heroin had ever been.

The only thing she'd never learned to do was to stop thinking about Adam. She couldn't have done that, even if she'd set her soul on it. Adam would always be a part of her, and that was a fact she didn't ever bother to challenge. He'd enriched her life immeasurably, had saved her from utter destruction. And if, in the end, his leaving had caused her a pain as sharp as a surgeon's knife, then that was something she had to accept.

There were no recriminations, no blame. He had done what he'd thought was right. That was how he'd always acted . . .

'Anyway,' said Margot, drifting out of her thoughts, 'from tomorrow on I have to cover the Theatre Festival fringe. Six ultra-modern plays, of which two don't even have scripts. If you think *that's* a bed of roses, I'll gladly swap you.'

'No, thanks,' Eddie shuddered. 'That's above and beyond the call of duty, I agree.' He laid his hand on hers, leaving it there just a fraction too long. 'Meant to tell you—I've got tickets for *Aida* tonight. Up in the gods, but Maria Scalabrino is singing.'

'I can't, Eddie,' she said regretfully. 'I'm going up to see Mum and Carl, straight from work.'

His face fell. 'Can't you put them off?'

'I promised,' she said gently. He was about to insist, so she had no choice but to tell him. 'It's my birthday.'

He stared at her for a moment, then threw his napkin down angrily. 'God damn!'

She could only say, 'I'm sorry, Eddie.'

'Why don't you *tell* me anything? You keep everything to yourself, Margot, like some kind of mysterious being who's above human contact. I mean, maybe I'd have liked to buy you a birthday present, make the day special for you——'

'I didn't want a present,' she said soothingly. 'And the day is special. I'm out of my teens at last.'

'It's special for you,' he said bitterly. 'But you obviously don't want to share it with me. You probably wouldn't even have told me if I hadn't asked you about *Aida*.'

'I didn't want any fuss,' she said firmly. She'd known Eddie would buy her an expensive present, and that would only have complicated things between them. 'Please don't get me anything. I really don't want any presents.'

'You don't want any commitments, you mean.' He pushed his plate away as though he'd lost his appetite. 'And you don't want to give any. Is that how you intend to live the rest of your life? The Ice Maiden, drinking orange juice and nibbling lettuce?'

'Don't spoil my birthday,' she smiled.

'I wish I knew what happened to you in that mysterious past of yours,' growled Eddie. 'I've got a hunch some man hurt you really badly. I'd like to knock his brains out, whoever the swine is.'

'Nobody hurt me,' Margot soothed him, reflecting that Adam would tower over Eddie Grant by at least a foot. There was a great deal that Eddie didn't know about her. Like the fact that she'd once been a heroin addict. 'And I'm sorry about *Aida*. Why not ask Gloria Holmes—she loves opera.'

'That wouldn't make you jealous?' he asked drily.

'Of course not.'

'Of course not,' Eddie grunted. 'OK, I'll ask Gloria. Happy birthday, Prescott.'

'Thanks.' Margot continued to eat in tranquil serenity despite Eddie's wounded silence. She was looking forward to tonight. Since she'd got back to London, relations with her mother and Carl had improved dramatically, almost magically. The change in her personality had seemed almost miraculous to them, but they'd accepted it joyfully. They didn't know about the heroin, or about Adam Korda.

Adam was a secret she kept to herself. She hadn't even told Gill Reynolds, who'd cried with relief when Margot had told her she was off heroin. The few people who knew she'd been an addict understood only that she'd gone to stay with a friend in the country to de-tox. They also knew that there was no chance, ever, that Margot Prescott would touch any sort of drug with a bargepole again. Her distaste extended even to alcohol, as Eddie had complained.

'Want to go riding this weekend?' Eddie asked, offering an olive-branch.

'Great,' she said with animation. Adam had left her with a lasting love of horses, and she'd been riding as often as she could, enjoying the exercise which took her effortlessly back to Harcourt.

'I love to see you on a horse,' said Eddie. 'You look just right in the saddle, as though you'd been riding all your life. You're so graceful, so beautiful, Margot. Sometimes I think——'

'Look at the time!' She tilted her slender wrist to show him her watch. She felt desperately sorry for Eddie, but she didn't want to give him any encouragement at all. If only he could keep his feelings to friendship ... 'We'd better hit the trail in a few minutes,' she smiled. 'Eat your chips up.'

The evening at Purley was pleasantly relaxed. In the years after her mother's remarriage, Margot had become almost a stranger to her. She hadn't begrudged her mother the happiness and fulfilment she'd found with Carl and her new children, but she'd felt then that there was nothing in common between them any more.

Now she felt differently. She was growing to respect Carl, learning to love her new sister and brother. Learning that there was more in common between her and her mother than she'd imagined.

She left her mother's house at around eleven, and drove back through North London to her new flat in Barnet. She'd been glad to get away from her old digs, which had had a sad, haunted atmosphere after she'd come down from Harcourt. The flat made up for its high rent by being clean, pleasant, and having a walled garden where Margot was able to sunbathe on warm weekends. But it was infinitely different from the majesty and peace of Harcourt. She was thinking about Darkrising Wood as she locked her Mini. She'd watched it through the glory of autumn, and into the stark drama of winter. By now, she knew, it would be in glorious leaf, the earth carpeted with bluebells and celandines.

She had a vision of Adam, riding Macallen through Darkrising, his lean body moving in perfect harmony with the stallion's. She could almost hear the rustle of leaves underfoot, smell the rich fresh smell of the earth. Did he ever think of her? Wonder how she was?

Did he ever guess that she had never stopped loving him, had never stopped thinking about him?

She unlatched the door, stooping to pick up the morning's post. Ten or twelve birthday cards, mostly from old school-friends. One, though, was different.

She tore it open quickly. There was no signature, just three lines of distinctive black handwriting on the heavy white card, and something small wrapped in a fold of tissue:

> Happy birthday, pearl. So you're all grown up. You've stopped falling in rivers . . . or so it seems? Take care of yourself.

In the fold of tissue was a confection of tiny speckled feathers, beautifully tied in the shape of a small insect. The needle-sharp hook pricked her finger slightly as she lifted it out. A salmon fly.

She sat down in the hallway, midway between a laugh and a sob. The memories had come flooding back in a rush, the intense sweetness of that afternoon in the river . . .

The poise that had so infuriated Eddie Grant this morning was suddenly gone. What on earth would he say if he could see his Ice Maiden right now, crying helplessly over a fish-hook?

She brushed her wet eyelids with her wrists, looking down at the fly, lying on the blurred words. Those terse lines said so much to her. They said, 'I'm missing you. I think of you. I haven't forgotten.'

It was the first sign she'd had from Adam in four months, and it had moved her unexpectedly. The fierce ache she'd fought so hard to conquer was back again, filling her heart with longing for Adam. It would take a long time to die down again.

She made herself a cup of tea, and went straight to her cluttered desk. It was late, but her letter to him couldn't wait. She'd almost got to the bottom of the page before she crumpled it up, and tossed it miserably into the waste-paper basket. Emotional, all-too-transparent words, full of a passion that was painfully obvious.

Exactly the kind of thing that would most put him off any further contact. He'd been brutally clear about not wanting any further displays of sentiment from her. *Forget about me, for God's sake*, he had commanded, when they'd parted for the last time. *We need a long, long break from each other. Get yourself together, now. Go out and shine, pearl.*

Well, she'd begun to shine. She could look back over the past few months, without false vanity, and see that her whole life had been transformed. She'd done what Adam had wanted her to do, and she knew that from his eyrie up in Darkrising, he would be watching her career with some kind of satisfaction. The very fact that he'd sent her this note at all proved that.

She'd wanted to write so many times, to try and thank him, try and show him how deep her feelings of gratitude went.

But that, too, had been forbidden.

She touched the heavy card with her fingertips. Maybe he didn't want any kind of reply at all. Yet that tiny little hook was such a potent symbol for both of them. What the hell was it? A message that he hadn't managed to get her out of his mind? A reminder to stay free and unattached, swimming in the stream?

It was a complex, enigmatic gesture from so positive a man. Maybe she was being too complicated. Maybe the message was just a simple 'forget me not'.

Margot put her pen down, and stared ahead with dark, absent eyes, remembering that rainy autumn day when he'd first walked into her life. The leaves blowing in the deserted car park, the tall man with the compelling grey eyes opening the door of the Mercedes for her . . .

She hadn't had the slightest inkling what had lain in store for her. How could she have anticipated the ordeal that was to lead to love—and in the end, to a loneliness more intense than any she'd known before.

Oh yes, it was true that she now had more friends than she'd ever had. Adam had taught her to free herself from the anger and resentment that had made her adolescent years so turbulent, and as her true personality expanded, people were drawn to her for almost the first time in her life. Since Harcourt, she had more friends, more male suitors, than she needed.

Yet she knew in her heart that she could never give herself fully to any of them. There was only one friend, one lover, whom she truly desired. And without him, would she ever learn to be truly happy, behind that Mona Lisa smile?

She didn't send any kind of reply in the end, not then, nor

during the weeks that followed. She judged that Adam wouldn't want a response, not then. It was cruelly hard to have to remain silent; but she desperately wanted to hear from him again. And the only chance she had of hearing from Adam was to respond as coolly as possible to him . . .

As the summer season got under way, her workload was getting heavier. Her brief called for no more that a few articles a week, yet it was extraordinary how much work went into those columns. There was a lot more pressure than in the *City News* days, Lawrence Sweetney expected a great deal from her.

It wasn't that she didn't relish the pressure, and thoroughly enjoy giving of her best in a difficult brief; but knowing that the *Herald* had a British and international readership of two million sometimes still daunted her.

May became June, with a flood of showers. Wednesdays and Thursdays became heavier than usual for her, when Lawrence Sweetney introduced a special Friday supplement, where she had a chance to really shine. The Friday edition, which was full of West End theatre and concert ads, had more young readers than any other, and that added to the stimulus of providing a responsible guide.

The second week in June brought hot weather at last. Thursday promised to be a scorcher. The office was almost always quiet in the early mornings, and because she wasn't bound by the same deadlines as news reporters, she was able to take advantage of the comparative calm.

But by midday, the pace was starting to pick up, in preparation for what Eddie called the feeding frenzy of early evening.

Her eyes drifted around the rapidly filling office. She was looking forward to her squash game. With a smile, she remembered her mother's first reaction when she'd come to see Margot at work: 'Somehow I had the idea you'd have a room of your own!'

The office stretched from one side of the building to the other, almost entirely lined with windows. Thirty or more desks filled the main space, most of them occupied. The air was filled with noise—typewriters, electronic printers, telex machines, the hum of voices, the ringing of telephones. 'Nobody has a room of their own here,' she'd smiled ruefully at her mother.

Eddie picked her up at twelve, and they walked the few hundred yards down Fleet Street to the mews where the Lancaster Sporting Club was discreetly tucked away.

The game was lively, especially for the initial half-hour. 'My point,' Eddie said with satisfaction, mopping his face with the sweatband on his wrist. 'You're not concentrating, Prescott.'

'Sorry.' Margot bent to touch her toes, stretching her long legs. In the ultra-short white skirt and top, she looked delicious—tanned, feminine and healthy. Eddie was watching her, and she met his eyes, seeing the desire in them. In the past few weeks his feelings for her had obviously intensified, the way she'd known they would do. Her heart sank slightly at his expression. She didn't *want* an intense relationship with Eddie. 'Come on,' she said briskly. 'Your service.'

He served hard into the corner, and Margot had to scramble to return it. It was useless for her to try and defeat Eddie by matching his power strokes. She had to rely on her sharper reflexes and greater agility, and outfox him with deceptive play.

It was time she changed her tactics. She flicked his volley high into the corner, with a lightness of touch which made it drop down almost vertically. Eddie pounced forward with a little grunt of effort, but fumbled the shot, and she was on hand to pat it across the court, out of reach.

'Damn,' he muttered as she walked gracefully across the wooden floor. 'Should have kept my mouth shut.'

'It's hot,' puffed Margot. A sheen of sweat gleamed on her tanned forearms, but she was relishing the feeling of energy and health that was flowing along her veins. 'Summer must be here at last.'

'Hope it's better than last summer.' He dashed to return her service, and for an intense half-minute they played without speaking, only the crash and echo of their game breaking the silence.

'Oh, for Pete's sake!' he gasped at last, not even bothering to go for her final shot. 'You're getting too good for me.' He held his sides, panting, then walked over for his towel. 'You're right, I should lay off the booze. I'm giving you ten years and five stone already.'

She smiled at him, swinging her racket idly, then followed his upward gaze.

In the normally deserted gallery up above them, a tall man was standing, leaning on the railing.

Adam.

CHAPTER NINE

MARGOT's heart flipped right over inside her. Adam Korda hadn't been out of her mind for five months, and yet it was like seeing him for the first time. She could only stare up into the brilliant depths of those magnificent, dangerous grey eyes. His smile was slow, almost teasing, but he gave no sign of recognition.

'Someone you know?' Eddie asked tightly, his hackles instantly rising.

'A friend.' Her mouth was dry, her knees weak as water. Suddenly, she wanted badly to sit down. 'Hello,' she said quietly to Adam. 'Nice to see you.'

'Likewise.' Adam looked lean and hard, as though he'd lost weight. But there was no lessening of vigour in the honey-tanned, intensely masculine face. 'Who's winning?'

'The score's even,' Margot told him. Her heart was thudding heavily against her ribs, and she seemed unable to take her eyes off Adam.

Eddie Grant spun the racket in his hand, his face reddening slightly. 'Shall we get on with our game, Prescott?' he suggested grimly. He glanced up at Adam with a sour expression. 'We've only got the court for another ten minutes,' he explained pointedly.

'I wouldn't miss the game for worlds,' Adam purred.

With a supreme effort, Margot dragged her attention back to the game. Squash had suddenly become utterly irrelevant. Next to the presence of the tall, dark man in the gallery above, just about everything was irrelevant.

She served numbly, only to have Eddie slam a return across the court, making her scramble. She could feel Adam's eyes on her, and she cursed inwardly, her mind seething with questions. What was he doing here? Had he come to find her? Obviously he had. But of all the times for him to be watching her, hot and tumble-haired, and scuttling across a squash court——

She won the point by sheer unconscious luck. Judging by Eddie's face, he was in none too good a mood. A blind man couldn't have missed her reaction to Adam's arrival; and of all the men in the world, Adam was probably the most likely to bring out latent feelings of insecurity in another man!

Her body finished the game for her, on autopilot. Her awareness was focused on Adam's presence up above; and far from concentrating on Eddie's increasingly violent strokes, all she could think about was what might be going on in Adam's mind as he watched her.

'Game to you,' snarled Eddie at last. Margot was barely aware of having won. She glanced up at Adam, who applauded silently, and with that old hint of irony. The next players were already hovering expectantly at the back of the court.

'Who the hell's that?' Eddie challenged her in a low voice as they pushed through the door and walked up the stairs to the gallery.

'An old friend,' she said lightly. 'I'll introduce you.'

'An ex-lover?' he interpreted, unsmiling. '*The* ex-lover?'

'He's someone who was very kind to me, Eddie.'

He snorted disbelievingly, but had no time to say anything further. They met Adam at the top of the stairs. He was formally dressed in a dark three-piece suit, and he looked magnificent, his sheer physical presence dominating everything around him.

'Well played,' he said gently, taking her hand. His kiss was not on her lips, but on the damp skin of her temple, an achingly familiar touch.

'Eddie, this is Adam Korda. Adam, this is Eddie Grant.' He was still holding her hand. Margot was flushed and breathless, but not from the game. And Adam wasn't remotely interested in Eddie.

His gaze travelled up her figure with slow appreciation, finishing on her eyes. 'You've put on weight,' he said, in a tone of velvety intimacy that made the skin prickle down her spine. Eddie stiffened beside her, and she tried to sound light.

'You've lost weight,' she countered. 'What brings you to London?'

'This,' he said gently '. . . and that.' His eyes were so compelling, as clear and deep as rockpools. Eyes you could sink into, eyes you could lose yourself in. She tore her gaze away with a conscious effort of will, and he smiled, as though reading her turbulent emotions. 'You'll both need a shower,' he said, releasing her hand. 'I'll meet you in the restaurant afterwards.'

'Right,' Eddie said, taking Margot's arm in a painfully tight grip, and more or less hustling her along the gallery. 'Who the hell *is* he?' he demanded, before they were even out of earshot. He was obviously furious with her, both for beating him, and because of Adam. 'You looked at him as though he owns your soul!'

Not a bad guess, she thought drily. 'Adam's an old friend of my father's,' she explained patiently. 'He was very kind to me when I needed help.'

'Yeah? What's he do?'

'He breeds horses,' Margot smiled, which was probably the understatement of the year.

'He doesn't look the type,' grunted Eddie. 'So what's he doing here?'

'I don't know,' she said truthfully. 'You're hurting my arm, Eddie.'

'He's the one, isn't he?' Eddie accused her, eyes staring into hers from behind his tinted lenses. 'The one who hurt you, the one you can't forget———'

'Please, Eddie.' Why did he have to be here at all? she thought unreasonably. All she wanted right now was to be alone with Adam, without complications. The cruel truth was that Eddie, too, was irrelevant. 'We don't have too much time.'

'And you don't want to miss a minute of friend Adam's company?'

'I'm going to get my shower,' she said calmly, pulling her arm free of Eddie's grip. She walked into the women's changing-rooms, pulled off her clothes, and got into the white-tiled shower cubicle. She didn't have to fantasise today. Adam was out there, waiting for her. It was almost impossible to believe! Whatever the reasons, the one fact was inescapable. He'd come to find her. He was here.

She closed her eyes, aware that every inch of her tanned skin was prickling with a sensation that was half delight, half pain. That ache of love was starting in her, like a wound that nothing could ever heal except Adam's touch. *No emotion*, she reminded herself sharply. Control yourself, Margot! For God's sake don't drive him away by showing him just how much you adore him . . .

But there was an odd feeling in her heart, like the trembling of a butterfly's wings, that she hadn't felt since Harcourt.

She showered, washed and dried her hair, and dressed in record time. But as she walked into the plush dining-room, Eddie had already arrived, obviously determined not to let her have a minute alone with Adam.

Adam rose fluidly from the table he'd been sitting at, smiling at them both. 'That was quick. May I buy you both a drink?'

'You can't,' Eddie said shortly. 'Only members can buy drinks here.'

'I *am* a member,' Adam said. 'I've just been made one.'

'And how did you manage that so quickly?' Eddie asked ungraciously.

'I cheated,' Adam smiled. 'The Club Chairman happens to be an old friend of mine.'

'Sir Edward Ferrars?' said Eddie with barely veiled incredulity.

'I have two of his mares in my stables right now,' Adam said casually. 'They've both been served by my top stallion, Macallen.' The barest movement of an eyebrow had the waiter hurrying over to them. 'I've also taken the liberty of ordering lunch to be served in the next room, in about ten minutes,' he added. 'It's more private in there. Now, what will you have to drink?'

'I'll have a vodka and fresh orange,' Margot said hastily as Eddie's mouth set in a resentful line under his droopy moustache.

'I thought you never touched alcohol,' Eddie said sharply.

'Today I feel like a vodka and fresh orange,' she said sweetly, wishing to heaven Eddie would stop being so boorish. As if getting the message, Eddie subsided into the seat Adam waved him to, and decided he'd have his usual beer. Did Adam think Eddie was her lover? So damned hard to tell what he was thinking behind that handsome face. God forbid he should get the wrong idea about her relationship with Eddie Grant. Or was it, perhaps, for the best that Eddie was here—as a chaperon to stop her from saying or doing anything stupid?

'So what does bring you to London?' she asked Adam, trying to sound cool and poised. 'Business?'

'Yes. I went to meet some VIPs at Heathrow this morning,' he said. The lines round his eyes deepened in a quiet smile. 'Three brood mares from Hong Kong. I like to be on hand on these occasions, just to check that everything goes smoothly. They're in boxes, on their way to Harcourt right now.'

'All the way from Hong Kong! That's a long way to send three mares to stud,' said Margot in awe.

'A long way, and a lot of money,' Adam nodded. 'The owner, who's a Chinese millionaire, was determined on Macallen, despite all the difficulties. He's building up what he hopes will be one of the best strings of mares in the Far East. These three will be at Harcourt for the next two years, in which time they should have produced two foals each.'

'Just like that,' Eddie put in drily. 'Production-line horses?'

'If it all went as smoothly as a production line,' Adam said pleasantly, 'my life would be a lot easier.'

'And what happens if there isn't a result?'

'There's always a result,' Adam answered the aggressive question easily. He looked at Margot. 'I don't have to ask how your career's going. I read the answer every day in the *Herald*.'

'My stuff doesn't always have a by-line,' she said, to cover the way her cheeks had flushed.

'I seldom have any trouble spotting your work,' he smiled. The waiter arrived with their drinks, and after a few more moments' desultory chat, with Eddie looking more ominous by the minute, they moved to the little private dining-room next door. Margot was longing to ask Adam about Harcourt, about what the countryside looked like, whether the great Hall was furnished yet. But she couldn't. Eddie's presence inhibited any discussion that might reveal just how close she and Adam had been, and the circumstances of their months together. And the last thing Adam would want would be a display of unwelcome emotion from her.

The meal, which was mostly cold, and had obviously been specially prepared in their honour, was a long way from their usual self-service fare. Adam talked easily and entertainingly about the horses. If he was disturbed or amused by Eddie's glowering expression, he gave no sign of it. His charm made up for her own awkwardness and Eddie's sulks, and Margot watched him with adoring eyes.

He had definitely lost weight, she was sure of it; the lines of his cheekbones and jawline were harsher then she remembered. She wanted to ask him about that, too, but couldn't. She just watched him, thinking how unbelievably handsome he was, drinking in that potent aura he always exuded.

'I had another reason for coming down south,' Adam remarked over the excellent dessert. 'The Classic at Cheltenham tomorrow afternoon. Sail Away is the second favourite.'

'One of your horses?' Eddie grunted.

Adam nodded. 'The big liver chestnut. Remember him from Harcourt, Margot?' She nodded. 'I thought he'd make a promising flat racer once, but he's fulfilled himself as a steeplechaser. If you're a betting man, you might get quite good odds on him.'

'I'm not a betting man,' Eddie said flatly.

'Too bad,' said Adam with total indifference to the snub. He glanced at his watch, the glitter of diamonds bringing back so many memories for Margot. 'Time's getting on. I'm going to have to rush.'

Margot felt a physical pain lance through her. Was he going to just walk out of her life again, the way he'd so abruptly walked in? Tears were disastrously close beneath her calm expression now, and she put her hands in her lap to hide the fact that they'd suddenly started shaking badly.

Adam's eyes met hers, no smile in them now. 'I have a box at Cheltenham,' he said quietly. 'I thought you might like to come.'

Her heart jumped painfully at the invitation, making her unable to speak for a moment. With a supreme effort, she controlled her expression.

'I don't think I've got anything else on,' she said coolly. Eddie's silence was monumental, but she didn't give a damn right then. She was just too happy, and too busy trying to disguise it. 'Yes, I'd like to come.'

'Good,' said Adam, equally casually. 'You've never been to Cheltenham before, have you?'

'No.' She shook her dark head.

'I'll enjoy showing you round.' He glanced at Eddie. 'I'm sorry to have to leave you like this, but my afternoon is filled with rather boring business meetings.' Eddie didn't say a word, but Adam hardly seemed to notice. His eyes were back on hers. 'What time will you be free tomorrow?'

'Around twelve-thirty,' she told him.

'I'll pick you up then, at the *Herald* office.'

She nodded, not trusting herself to say anything else. In that brief pause before she'd agreed to go with him, she'd seen something in his eyes which she'd never seen there before. Something that was almost like pleading. Or was she being absurd?

Adam's departure was urbane, relaxed. Eddie watched him leave with an expressionless face, then leaned back, one arm stretched out along the chair-back.

'I must seem pretty second-rate after Adam Korda,' he said abruptly, with more than a touch of bitterness in his face and voice. She didn't know what to say, so she reached out a hand to him. He was in the same boat as she was right now, and there was just no solution for either of them. 'Oh, don't feel bad,' he said drily, and drained his glass. 'After all, you've given me enough signals, haven't you? You never wanted anything more from me than friendship, and I've been too stupid and too conceited to believe it.'

'Eddie, it isn't the way you think,' she said quietly. 'Adam isn't in love with me.'

'That's why he came all the way out here to find you, is it?' Eddie shrugged. 'It's immaterial, anyway. The point that concerns me is that you love him. You always have done, and you always will do.'

Margot flinched. 'Does it show?' she asked unhappily.

'The fact that you try and hide it shows.' Eddie smiled without amusement. 'He's quite a man, Margot. I can see why he'd be hard to forget. I wish you luck.'

'What with?' she asked.

'With your dream,' he said, eyes gentle now behind the tinted lenses. 'Everybody has a dream in this life, Margot. Making it come true is usually the difference between a life fulfilled, and a life wasted in useless longings. Yours happens to be called Adam Korda. Shall we go?'

She was silent on the way back to the office, her mind filled with unhappy thoughts about Adam, mingled with more mundane concerns, like when she'd have the time to buy a new dress for Cheltenham.

As they turned into Fleet Street, she touched Eddie's arm gently. She had to lift her voice over the noise of the traffic. 'I'm sorry, Eddie,' she said, pitying him.

'Don't be,' he answered, looking up at the blue sky between the buildings. 'I always knew that another man was number one in your heart. I just thought that in time you'd settle for a number two. Now I know better, that's all. You'll never be happy with any other man, Margot. Never.'

The horses poured over the fence, a torrent of glossy, muscular bodies, filling the air with the thunder of their hooves, the jockeys' colours blazing against the emerald turf.

Margot had been holding her breath in a mixture of awe at the glory of the sight, and horror at the naked danger of it all. In a matter of a second or two, almost all the horses were over; then, one of the tail-enders was taking the fence awkwardly, disaster written in every straining line.

The horse landed with his head low, his forelegs crumpling, and she heard the jockey's gasp, quite clearly above the pounding of the receding field, as he thumped into the grass, and rolled over, trying to cover his head from the steel-shod hooves.

'Adam!' she said urgently, fingers digging into his arm.

'He's only winded,' Adam said unsympathetically. The jockey rose groggily to his feet, helped by two St John Ambulance men, while a small posse of helpers trotted to harness his equally dazed-looking mount. 'The idiot might have killed himself—and the horse. Good thing the going's soft.' He swung his fieldglasses to follow the stream of horses along the curve of the track, and over the next immaculate white and green fence.

She clung close to his hard strength, her fears for the jockey somewhat abated. It was a glorious day, and she couldn't remember when she'd last felt so alive, so happy.

'I had no idea it was so fast, so—*exciting*,' she said breathlessly. 'It's marvellous! Just listen to the crowd . . .'

'This is what it's all about,' Adam smiled, passing her the fieldglasses. 'All those thousands of people, shouting for their bets. That's how a horse can end up worth tens of millions of pounds.'

She followed the field, which was beginning to spread out as it reached the half-way mark. It was a beautiful sight, eight of the finest horses in Europe, thundering across velvety English turf, under the deep blue canopy of an English summer sky.

The slight breeze tugged at Margot's soft, wide hat, threatening to tip it off. She was wearing the outfit she'd bought the day before after work, in a pale cream that was almost white, set off with a silk scarf the deep blue of a summer sky. She looked and felt marvellous on this day. Cheltenham was thronged with people for the first race of the afternoon.

She and Adam had arrived about half an hour ago, and had gone straight to the members' enclosure to meet a small group of Adam's friends. His sisters hadn't arrived yet, but Sail Away wasn't going to be racing for another hour, in the big race of the afternoon.

The noise of the crowd rose to a roar as the horses approached the final fence. There were only five left by now, with two in contention for first place. To Margot's untrained eye they were neck-and-neck as they flew past the winning-post, but the tall woman in her fifties, whom Adam had introduced as Lady Warrender, gave a whoop of delight.

'Tour de France, by a head! I've just won ten pounds!'

Adam grinned at Margot. He was wearing the fawn Burberry he'd worn the first day they'd met—as a very private joke between them, she suspected. During the drive up from London, he'd talked casually about Harcourt, describing the beauty of the countryside in summer; but the only hint of any more personal contact had been the way he'd taken her arm so possessively among the crowds.

Her impression that he'd lost weight seemed to be mistaken today. He looked as fit and potent as he'd ever done, and as handsome as Lucifer. The grey eyes met hers with that old, old magic, making her heart jump in reaction. Then he glanced over her shoulder. 'Ah,' he said. 'Here comes the Korda clan.'

Margot turned to be introduced to the three people who'd just arrived. Adam's two sisters, both in wide-brimmed hats like her own, were in their mid-twenties, a few years older than Margot herself. Vanessa, the eldest, was surprisingly fair and rosy-cheeked, and had the air of a comfortable country squire's wife, an impression borne out by her jovial, tweed-suited husband, Philip.

Charmian, who was on her own, was more like Adam. Tall and dark-haired, she moved with born aristocratic grace, and she had Adam's heart-warming smile.

All three greeted Margot with unexpected warmth, yet she sensed something else, too. Curiosity, an appraisal, perhaps, which Charmian made the least effort to hide.

'What a beautiful suit,' was the first thing she said to Margot. 'You look so cool and fresh!'

'How's Sail Away today?' Vanessa's husband Philip asked Adam. 'Looking fit?'

'He was in a bit of a lather last time I saw him,' smiled Adam. 'He gets nervous on the big day sometimes.'

'I hope he's not going to lose me my stake,' Vanessa sighed. 'I've put twenty pounds on him.'

'What odds?' Adam wanted to know.

'Seven to four,' she grimaced. 'I'm always too late,' she complained to Margot. 'By the time I get my bet on, the odds have narrowed down to the pitch where it's scarcely worth putting anything on.'

'Twenty quid may be scarcely anything to you,' snorted Charmian, 'but it's a fortune to me.'

'Charmian runs a small plant nursery,' Adam explained. 'I've tried to help her out, but she's too proud to take my money, so she works fifteen hours a day, and lives on crusts.'

'What sort of plants?' Margot asked, smiling.

'Hardy annuals,' Charmian replied. 'Are you interested in gardening?'

'I love it,' nodded Margot, and saw Charmian's expression change to pure pleasure.

'Good. We'll have lots to talk about.' She turned to Adam. 'Let's go to the box, big brother. I'm half-starved!'

'Hope you've laid on your usual spread, Adam,' Vanessa said with relish. 'We've come all the way from Norfolk, and we're starving.' She took Margot's arm in a motherly way. 'Are you interested in racing, Margot? Or does the whole thing bore you to tears?'

'It certainly doesn't bore me,' she smiled. All the Kordas had grey eyes, she thought. Although it was Charmian who most immediately reminded her of Adam, her face was of an entirely different cast from her brother's, feminine and delicate. She had flanked Margot's other side, leaving Philip and Adam to bring up the rear with Lady Warrender and the rest of the party. Inquisitive sisterly attention to the new female arrival, she thought wryly, and didn't blame them. How many times had they seen women come and go in Adam's crowded life? Yet it was no effort to chat easily with them, and before they'd got to the box, she'd decided quite firmly that she liked them both.

The box was, to Margot, astonishingly grand. It had a splendid view of the track, and a mouthwatering cold lunch had been laid out on a buffet against one wall, with a dozen bottles of champagne on ice, and what looked like several crates more under the table.

Adam was still involved in a highly technical discussion of breeding merits with some of his other guests, so she and his sisters moved easily into the role of hostesses.

She met Adam's eyes again as she passed him a plate, and felt that pang of desire shoot through her. How sweet it would be to be always at his side, loving him, helping him . . .

As soon as all the plates had been loaded, and glasses filled, Charmian led Margot out on to the balcony, away from the crowd. They sat together, looking out over the colourful scene down below.

'There,' sighed Charmian. 'Out of the mêlée. Do you mind if I ask how old you are?'

Margot fielded the unexpected question as neatly as she could. 'I turned twenty last month.'

'You're very poised for twenty,' the other woman smiled. 'I'm twenty-six, by the way.' The intelligent grey eyes were assessing her unambiguously now, drifting from her face to her hands. 'Forgive me, Margot. I know a little bit about you. So does Vanessa. We know that you spent most of the winter at Harcourt with Adam, and we think we know why.'

Margot felt her cheeks colour, but she didn't look away. 'I owe my life to your brother, Charmian,' she said quietly.

'Was it as bad as that?' Charmian sipped her champagne thoughtfully, then put the glass down. 'We had some idea, though Adam has always been exceptionally good at keeping his private life private—even from his sisters.' She smiled again, apologetically. 'He told us the bare minimum of course. We've also read your article in *Liberty*, which helped to flesh out what Adam told us. You've been exceptionally brave.'

'I was exceptionally lucky,' Margot corrected. 'If Adam hadn't stepped into my life, I'd probably be lying in a gutter somewhere right at this moment.'

'That's very hard to believe.' Charmian's eyes drifted over Margot's creamy-white suit. 'Addiction's the last thing I'd ever have expected in you.'

'I've changed rather significantly since last year,' Margot replied with a wry smile. 'Though I don't blame you for expecting me to be absolutely awful!'

'We weren't expecting that, either.' Charmian shook her dark head. 'Having read your work, and having heard something about your life from Adam, we were expecting someone charming, sensitive, and formidably intelligent.' She smiled slightly. 'Vanessa and I are just country bumpkins, Margot. You'll find us very dull, I'm afraid. But we do have warm hearts.'

'That's obvious,' said Margot with an embarrassed expression. 'You're very kind.' She picked at her food. 'Do you want to know exactly what happened?'

'No. That's between you and Adam.' Careful eyes probed her expression. 'But you don't bear Adam any sort of—grudge?'

'Of course not!' said Margot, dark eyes widening in surprise. 'Why should I bear him a grudge?'

'You've been through a painful ordeal,' Charmian said obliquely. 'According to Aileen Bell, Adam more or less kidnapped you, and held you captive at the gamekeeper's lodge. She felt you'd been very harshly treated. Is that true?'

'I treated Mrs Bell fairly harshly myself,' Margot replied with a half-smile. 'At least, I did at first. Adam was very forceful, yes. I wouldn't recommend it as a blanket cure for addiction, but in my case——' She shrugged, picking up a chicken wing. 'It happened to be exactly what I needed. I'll always be in Adam's debt. Why should you think I was angry with him?'

'Adam's too damned forceful by half,' Charmian said with a frown. 'It makes my blood run cold sometimes. Don't tell Vanessa—she's got a particularly vivid imagination. Did he really snatch you off the pavement——?' She broke off, shaking her head. 'I'm sorry. I really don't want to pry into what happened between you and Adam.'

'That's all right,' Margot said easily. Charmian took off her wide-brimmed hat, and dropped it beside her. She hadn't touched her food yet.

'Given your situation,' she went on, 'I'm sure Adam would have told you about our brother Michael. About his cancer, his addiction.'

'And his death,' Margot said quietly. She put her plate down, her appetite suddenly gone. 'Yes, he told me. I'm very sorry.'

'You've had your own tragedy,' Charmian said gently, 'so you understand.' Margot wondered absently how much exactly Adam's sisters knew about her. 'I was eighteen when it happened,' Charmian went on, 'and Vanessa was nineteen. Adam was twenty-four.' She stared out across the sunlit track. 'You have to understand that Adam became the head of our family when our parents died. He was more than a brother to us he was our father and mother, too. He took all the responsibility—and he took most of the pain.'

'He's rather good at that,' Margot said softly.

'Yes,' Charmian agreed. 'He is. Adam's the closest thing I know to the perfect man. But then,' she smiled, 'I am his sister. It was Adam who took most of the brunt of Michael's tragedy. He managed to shelter us all in some strange way, even Michael himself. But it hit him hard, and it took him a long time to get over it, nearly two years.'

Margot closed her dark eyes, leaning her head back against the fabric of the chair. Love for Adam was an ache in her, a gaping hole somewhere inside. 'Why are you telling me this?' she asked.

'I'm not sure.' Charmian leaned forward slightly, her expression serious. 'Maybe because there's something about the way Adam's been these past few months that reminds me of the way he looked when Michael died.'

'What do you mean?' asked Margot sharply, opening her eyes.

'Well, for a start, he's lost a lot of weight recently. I expect you noticed that.'

'Yes,' Margot said shortly.

'He seems so moody. Vanessa went up to stay with him two months ago, and she was quite troubled. He's withdrawn and depressed, which isn't like him. Oh, it doesn't show when he's got people around him,' she added, as Margot glanced uneasily back through the door at Adam's tall figure. 'Adam's always been very good at hiding his real feelings, even from his sisters. But this time he can't quite manage. He's even neglecting the stud, and you know how much the horses mean to him.'

'Yes,' Margot said again, in a low voice.

'That's why I'm so glad to be able to meet you. To see whether there's anything you could do that might help.'

'Me!'

'This has happened to him since you left Harcourt,' Charmian explained practically. 'Adam's always been surrounded by women, but they've never seemed to mean anything to him. Maybe this time it's different.'

Margot stared blankly, for the first time beginning to realise what Charmian was getting at. 'Are you saying— you think that Adam's pining away for *me*?'

'Is that so unlikely?'

'Oh, Charmian!' The irony would be amusing if it weren't so damned painful. The idea that Adam was missing her, brooding over her absence, had shaken her emotions up in an unwelcome way. She'd been determined to just enjoy today for its own sake, without brooding over her own problems. 'Do you think I walked out on him?'

Charmian spread her hands. 'Well . . .'

Margot took a deep breath to control her feelings, and spoke in a low voice. 'I didn't walk out on Adam, Charmian. If you must know, I care more about your brother than anything in the world.'

Charmian's grey eyes darkened. 'Then why——?'

'Adam sent me away from Harcourt. I think his motives

were irreproachable—but it was *he* who sent *me* away, not the other way around.' She met the other woman's eyes. 'He knew I was falling in love with him, and he felt that it was a dangerous infatuation that was best scotched in the bud. So he made me come back to London. For my own safety.'

'Ah.' Charmian's curving mouth eased into a bitter-sweet smile. 'I might have guessed. I might have guessed. Suddenly I feel sorrier for you than for Adam. He really is impossibly quixotic sometimes.' She searched Margot's now pale, beautiful face. 'I take it that your love for him is as strong as it ever was?'

'It hasn't changed,' Margot said drily.

Charmian was still staring at her as Adam and two of the other guests came out on to the balcony with a flood of conversation and laughter. Margot felt Adam's strong fingers close round her wrist, and looked up into his smiling, tanned face.

'If you've finished stuffing yourself,' he murmured, 'it's time I went to see Sail Away and my jockey before the off. Want to come?'

'Yes, please!' With a quick glance at Charmian, Margot rose to follow Adam out of the box, her heart pounding in her chest.

The parade ring was crowded. Most of the horses had already arrived, and the air was almost crackling with excitement. Margot and Adam stood with the diminutive jockey, watching Sail Away prance across the turf. Billy Shaughnessy, Adam's head trainer, was with them, too.

As Adam had said, the big liver chestnut horse's coat was dark with sweat. The lad who was trotting him was having some trouble restraining him; he was tossing his head against the bridle, and as they watched, he dug his front hooves in and kicked out backwards in the best bronco tradition, causing a scattering of spectators and other horses.

'He's a right pig today,' Billy said uneasily.

'He's just full of spirit,' Adam smiled. 'What do you think Kevin?'

The jockey balanced his helmet, goggles and whip in his hands, wizened face creasing. He was wearing the Korda colours, scarlet and gold, colours that were centuries old, Adam had once told her. They blazed in the sun, dazzling. 'He's best when he's nervous,' Kevin said shortly. 'We've got a good chance today.'

'That's what I think,' Adam agreed. Margot had been watching the television crew moving steadily their way, and now the interviewer slapped Adam familiarly on the shoulder.

'Hello, Adam. Spare us five minutes? Usual stuff.' Adam nodded, and moved off so that the camera could get the shimmering green of the track in the background.

Margot watched, listening absently to Billy telling her what a pig Sail Away could be. Her mind was still whirling with what Charmian Korda had told her. Was there really a chance that Adam had been missing her? That despite his dismissal of her five months ago, he'd never managed to get her out of his heart?

The thought brought an overwhelming wave of emotion washing through her, compounded of hope and tightening nerves. Adam stood tall in front of the cameras, the sunlight glinting among the dark curls of his hair. In every inch he was male, a superb animal at the very peak of his physical and mental powers. A man to make any woman dizzy.

She felt a fierce burn of pride run along her veins. He was magnificent. There was no other word for it. That he could be hers was a dream, as Eddie Grant had said, which might mean the difference between a life fulfilled and a life wasted ...

The signal was given for the jockeys to mount. Adam just got back in time to shake hands with Kevin.

'Good luck,' he said quietly.

'Thanks, Mr Korda.' He pulled on his helmet with a tense expression, and trotted off towards Sail Away. Adam slid his arm round Margot's waist, pulling her close. The gesture was exactly what she'd been longing for, and she laid her glossy head against his shoulder, feeling a security she hadn't known since the last time Adam had held her like this, at Harcourt.

'Is Sail Away all right?' she asked.

'He's going to win,' he said with complete confidence. She had to smile at him. If Adam said Sail Away would win, then he *would* win.

The horses had all mustered at the starting point, Sail Away still kicking nervously, earning his jockey a reprimand from the starter. 'Relax, Kevin,' Adam growled.

The noise of the crowd subsided expectantly for a moment. Then the tapes shot up, and the pack exploded into action with a roar from the stand. Magically, Sail Away was transformed from a nervous, jittery creature into an oiled thunderbolt on four speed-blurred hooves. With unerring power, he sought the lead, and by the time they were coming up to the first fence, he was ahead by two lengths.

Unexpectedly, Adam turned his back casually on the track, and walked with her across the parade ring grass.

'Don't you want to watch?' she asked in astonishment.

'Not particularly,' he smiled, looking down at her. 'You seem to get on well with my sisters.'

'They're very nice,' she nodded in puzzlement. 'Especially Charmian.'

'Yes. You were very thick with her out on the balcony.' His glance was veiled by lowered lashes. 'What were you talking about?'

'A-about horses,' Margot answered in confusion.

'Liar,' he said softly. 'Charmian's an interfering little minx.'

'What do you mean?' she asked unsteadily.

'I mean that I've got very sharp hearing. I was standing by the door, pretending to listen to Lisa Warrender,' he replied. 'And I couldn't help overhearing the last part of what you were saying to my sister.'

'Oh!' Margot's face flushed hotly with colour as she recalled what she'd just said to Charmian. 'I—I don't know what to say——'

'Little pearl,' he said huskily, 'you know exactly what to say.' His strong arms reached for her, the way they'd done in a thousand dreams, and with a little sob of emotion, she melted against him, nestling in his protective embrace. His body was warm, his muscles sleek and potent against her.

'Adam,' she whispered, her voice barely audible above the roar of the stands, 'I've missed you so much . . .' He drew her upturned face slowly against his mouth. With intoxicating sweetness, she felt his lips brush her own.

And as her mouth yielded to the delicious, familiar tyranny of his kiss, joy seemed to flood her like a bursting dam. She closed her eyes in surrender, letting her head drop back so that her dark hair cascaded away from her

forehead. His mouth tasted of champagne, his hands wer
cupping her face.

Nothing in the world mattered beyond this moment
not the eyes of a thousand watchers, not the thundering o
hooves, not the heat of the sun nor the inquisitive lens o
the television camera swinging their way.

Scarcely knowing whether she was dreaming o
waking, she looked up into the deep grey eyes that seeme
to look into her very soul, and as always, felt that electri
shock to the heart that she knew would never fade.

'You're so beautiful, pearl. The most beautiful woma
I've ever seen. That's what I thought, that very first day i
London, and it's what I think now.' He touched her parte
lips with gentle fingers, his expression wondering. 'Go
knows how I ever imagined I could live without you . .

'Then . . . You want me?' she said tremblingly, scarcel
daring to hope.

'Yes,' he nodded. 'I want you, Margot. For ever.'

'Adam . . .'

'I came to London to ask you to marry me, Margot.' H
smiled. 'I was going to do it tonight. Take you out, get yo
so tipsy that you couldn't say no. But my dear sister seem
to have accelerated things between us a little.'

'You don't have to get me tipsy,' Margot said. 'I'v
loved you since those first days at Harcourt, Adam. I wa
just withering away without you.'

'No reservations?' he asked quietly.

'None. I love you, don't you know that?'

The cheering of the crowd was rising to a peak, almo
drowning out the race commentary over the publi
address system. Sail Away's name could just be made ou
in the cacophony. Adam smiled down at her. 'I told yo
Sail Away would win,' he purred. 'How do you feel abou

being sequestered away in the country for the rest of your life, with several hundred successful racehorses—and me?'

'It overwhelms me,' she said truthfully. 'It's what I've dreamed of. Harcourt will always be my home, Adam. Anywhere else would be exile to me . . .'

'You're going to have to leave your wonderful new job,' he reminded her. 'Aren't you going to miss London and the bright lights? Miss your independence?'

'My independence!' she repeated wryly. 'It was desolation, Adam. And there isn't a single thing in my present life that I'll miss at Harcourt.' She looked up at him. 'I want your children, my love. I don't want to wait for them. And I've never believed in working mothers.'

'Children?' he asked with mock surprise. 'Wouldn't just one do?'

'A son to start with,' she promised him, 'but at least three or four, Adam. I'll have my way, you know I will.'

'Yes, pearl, I know you will.' He swept her up in his arms, laughing into her eyes with the triumph of a man claiming his woman, and for long minutes she was lost in him again, lost in the wonder of Adam.

'Adam,' she said breathlessly at last, 'look! They're about to finish!'

They both turned in time to watch the final few furlongs, their bodies pressed together. Sail Away was three lengths ahead, the scarlet and gold figure of Kevin hunched over the saddle. In the joy and triumph of the moment, Margot found herself willing the magnificent animal on with every fibre of her being.

He didn't falter. The rest of the field followed somewhat lamely in his wake as he raced past the white winner's post like the very personification of animal energy. And the crowd were wild with elation.

'There's a trophy,' smiled Adam. 'Shall we go and accept it?'

She was almost too weak on her legs to walk. She had to cling to Adam as they walked to the unsaddling enclosure, congratulations showering on them from all sides. On the balcony above, she caught sight of Charmian and Vanessa waving. Maybe it was the distance, but she thought Charmian's eyes looked wet with tears . . .

Colour, noise, the blaze of flashlights. Half dazed, she stood beside Adam, knowing only that she was radiantly happy. He'd come for her, again.

He'd come for her in the end, the way she'd always dreamed he would. Her ordeal of solitude was over. From now on Adam would always be there beside her, transforming her life, making it fulfilled, joyful, alive. She looked up at him, her face glowing in the sunlight.

'Why did you take so long?' she demanded, her voice pitched so that only he could hear.

'To be sure,' he told her. The cameras flashed and blazed as he dumped the golden trophy in her arms, and kissed her full on the lips, for twenty million viewers to see. 'To be sure that you could pick up the pieces of your life without me. To be sure that you wouldn't forget me, once our proximity was over.'

'Oh, Adam,' she sighed. 'And I thought you had faith in me!'

'From now on,' he vowed, 'you'll never leave my side.'

The dozens of television monitors around the paddock were all showing the same scenes. A big liver chestnut stallion flashing past the finishing post. And the figures of a man and woman, clinging together in a passionate kiss, oblivious to the world.

A picture repeated dozens of times around the paddock.

Countless numbers of times across countless numbers of screens. Just as it would be repeated countless times, with ever-deepening meaning and intensity, in their own happy lives.

Harlequin Presents

Coming Next Month

Available in November wherever paperback books are sold, or through
Harlequin Reader Service:

In the U.S.
901 Fuhrmann Blvd.
P.O. Box 1397
Buffalo, N.Y. 14240-1397

In Canada
P.O. Box 603
Fort Erie, Ontario
L2A 5X3

Take 4 books & a surprise gift FREE

SPECIAL LIMITED-TIME OFFER

Mail to   **Harlequin Reader Service**®

In the U.S.   In Canada
901 Fuhrmann Blvd.   P.O. Box 609
P.O. Box 1867   Fort Erie, Ontario
Buffalo, N.Y. 14269-1867 L2A 5X3

YES!   Please send me 4 free Harlequin Temptation® novels and my free surprise gift. Then send me 4 brand-new novels every month as they come off the presses. Bill me at the low price of $2.24 each*—a 10% saving off the retail price. There are no shipping, handling or other hidden costs. There is no minimum number of books I must purchase. I can always return a shipment and cancel at any time. Even if I never buy another book from Harlequin, the 4 free novels and the surprise gift are mine to keep forever.   142 BPX BP7F

*Plus 49¢ postage and handling per shipment in Canada.

Name   (PLEASE PRINT)

Address   Apt. No.

City   State/Prov.   Zip/Postal Code

This offer is limited to one order per household and not valid to present subscribers. Price is subject to change.   DOHT-SUB-1C

Taylor House

by Leigh Anne Williams

Enter the lives of the Taylor women of Greensdale, Massachusetts, a town where tradition and family mean so much. A story of family, home and love in a New England village.

Don't miss the Taylor House trilogy, starting next month in Harlequin American Romance with #265 *Katherine's Dream*, in October 1988, and followed by #269 *Lydia's Hope* and #273 *Clarissa's Wish* in November and December of 1988.

One house . . . two sisters . . . three generations

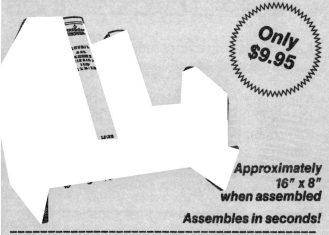

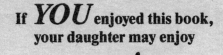